It Happened at the Park

Ryan Jo Summers

Published by
Satin Romance
An Imprint of Melange Books, LLC
White Bear Lake, MN 55110
www.satinromance.com

Cover Design by Fantasia Frog Designs

To God, for the gifts of humor and writing. And for giving me Ty, my collie, who prompted the introduction to the local dog park, which planted the seed for this story.
To fans of my previous books, thank you for coming back.

Acknowledgment:

To Pat Poreda, who came up with the title to this story, and to Pat and Walt Puckett, whose dogs provided me the inspiration for Tessa and Remi.

Chapter One

"Promise me."

Just hearing the urgent concern threaded through Cindy's voice made Cassidy cringe. Vainly she tried to push off her sister's earnest request with a laugh. It didn't work, falling pitifully flat.

"Promise me," Cindy persisted.

Sagging, Cassidy relented, bowing her head in quiet defeat. "Yes, of course. It won't be necessary, but I promise."

Satiated, Cindy leaned back, a peaceful smile on her face. It was the first one Cassidy had seen in days. Cindy was the realist of the family, whereas Cassidy refused to believe in any other outcome than the one she wanted. Hence the reason this whole discussion, and promise, were unnecessary. Except it made Cindy smile. That was enough.

Looking back now, their conversation had been something she overlooked the significance of. She'd missed it by a mile. Cindy had requested to see her, saying it was urgent, so she rescheduled the day's calendar and sandwiched Cindy in between two important meetings. Now, she had to admit she hadn't been willing to give her sister's concern the attention it deserved. Turns out, it was more important than her meetings.

Now, seated with her other sister, Karen, and Cindy's lawyer, and gazing at the thick file, she could not suppress the shivers claiming her. Despite the climate control of the room, goosebumps peppered her skin. Cindy had been the baby, youngest of the three sisters. How was anyone expected to think she would be the first to leave?

1

Cassidy thought back, before the meeting where she was obligated to make that promise. Cindy was the free spirit, the happy-go-lucky and most extroverted of the trio. She seldom had as much as a cold. No one imagined her getting sick, seriously sick. Least of all, Cassidy.

She still clearly pictured the day the three of them went to the beach for a weekend. Last year. Cindy had begged Cassidy and Karen to put their lives, jobs and family on hold to accompany her to what she called fulfilling her bucket list. She'd won the trip as part of a magazine sweepstakes prize and didn't want to go alone.

She sighed. That weekend at Rainbow Beach was as vivid in her mind as the beach's picturesque name. She closed her eyes, still seeing Cindy laughing and splashing in the waves in her new striped bikini, bought just for the trip. She'd thought the water too cold for swimming, but it never stopped Cindy. Cindy always laughed at life. Cindy's gift was the ability to see the humor in anything and bring others to see it as well.

Like the time Cindy made them rent horses and go riding. It was supposed to be fun, she'd promised, a gleam in her eye. It wasn't too bad until Karen got bucked off and landed in a big mud puddle. She'd only hurt her pride, lost the horse and had to ride back behind Cassidy. By the time they reached the stable, Karen's horse was waiting and they were laughing. The stable man thought they were crazy.

Karen said it took three washings to get all that dried mud out of her hair and clothes.

"So now it's settled," Higgins said, closing the file and breaking through Cassidy's memories. He gave her a long study before continuing. "It was quite simple and clean how Cindy wanted her assets dispensed and her remains handled. Do either of you have any questions?"

Yes, she had countless, but only one this guy could answer. She cleared her throat. "I still don't understand why I have to take them. Personally, Karen is much better suited for this." She flicked a wrist at her older sister. "She's already a mom so what's a couple more?"

Higgins pulled his glasses off. "That may be, Miss Grant. However, your sister determined you were the better guardian for them."

"Allergies," Karen cut in. "Don't forget about the allergies."

Like she could. What a convenient excuse. "But I work crazy long hours. They will never see me. I'll never see them. And it's unfair to expect me to do all that stuff Cindy listed." Truly, the promise was the short part. The following laundry list was exhaustive. She'd seen business contracts and budgets that were shorter.

Higgins eased out a sigh. "That may be as well, but unless you want to contest the will, and turn it over to probate to eventually decide upon, your best option really is to fulfill your promised obligation to your late sister."

That stupid promise, made under duress, on a tight schedule, in Cindy's room. What had she been thinking? Like normal, she hadn't been. Cindy had a penchant for making her brain freeze like she was eating ice cream too fast. "Fine. So where are they?" She was acutely aware of Karen's quiet smirk and Higgins' satisfied mile. She thrust her hand out for the records of her new charges.

"Happy Days Daycare. Directions are on that top page."

Half an hour later, and still lamenting silently over the legal facts, and that stupid promise, Cassidy pulled her BMW convertible into the Happy Days parking lot. Looking around, she felt dismay, and a little disgust, filling her. Picking up her phone, she dialed Karen's number.

"I'm here at Happy Days. Did you know what this place is like? And I haven't made it out of the car yet. The noise is deafening. Everyone here is running around, drooling and carrying on. I swear they all have rabies."

"Yes, I took them there, remember? Just take a big breath, march in there and claim them. I mean, they are your niece and nephew."

"Very funny, Karen." Why was she the lucky one to have all the allergies? Entirely too convenient.

"This is only a primer of what is ahead, Cassidy. Just think of all the things you will have to do now."

Cassidy had done nothing since she left the lawyer but think about her laundry list. Eyeing the building, she felt her brows pull up into a scowl. That would only add wrinkles. "You're no help. Good bye." Dropping the phone in her bag, she clutched both it and the file from the lawyer and pushed the door open with the toe of her heel. For Cindy, she would do this. Primer? Ha, she'd show Karen. Really, how hard could this be?

Within moments of introducing herself, Cassidy gazed in dismay. Squaring her shoulders, she studied the situation analytically. Okay, the smaller one was Tessa, and the larger one was Remi. She was positive of that before it was pointed out to her. Once the ponytailed daycare employee removed them from the mats in their play pen, they settled down and gave her a curious exam. Were they missing their mommy? Were they wondering why she was here instead of Cindy?

Another employee told her about their recent escapades and yet another brought out their stuff. Endless stuff. Toys, beds, clothing, food, snacks, where did it all end? She would have to put the top up on the convertible. Two bouncing ponytails helped her take it all to the car, both offering their condolences for Cindy. Cassidy could see Cindy had been a favorite mom at Happy Days Daycare.

She filled the BMW's trunk with as much of their stuff as she could, cramming more in the narrow back space. That left only the front seat for Tessa and Remi. She cringed as she pictured the mess they were going to make on the upholstery and glass.

Watching the Ponytails kneel and give final hugs and kisses to Tessa and Remi, and their own eager interactions, Cassidy was struck by how little attention she ever paid them. These were the loves of Cindy's life and she knew next to nothing about them. Did that make her a bad sister? Or as Karen put it, a bad auntie?

"Okay, guys, let's go," she said, holding the passenger door open for them. She shook hands with the Ponytails, thanked them for their excellent care and assured them she would fill in for Cindy the best she could. Leaving the deafening thunder of Happy Days in her rear view, she glanced at the two subdued dogs huddled on her seat.

Chapter Two

Ethan stretched, his arm nudged by a wet nose. He smiled at the hopeful whine at his ear.

"Hey, buddy, good morning." Warn sunshine splashed across his face as he opened his eyes to the comical expression on Jake's brown and black face. "I wish I could capture that look for the cartoons, Jake. Your morning expression kind of reminds me of the way some of our city's finest appear all day." Ruffling the dog's lop-sided ears, he stretched again, rolling out of bed. "Okay, gimme a minute and I'll get your breakfast."

He'd only had Jake four months, but he was already crazy about the mutt. Cruising the aisles at the shelter, he stumbled upon the lanky husky, shepherd, hound and whatever else he was mixed with. It had been instant attraction for both of them. He knew this was going to last longer and be better than the previous attraction he had to old whatshername. The chick who heavily discouraged him from having a dog again, citing various ridiculous reasons, and then ultimately left him anyway.

He must have been tripping or something when he thought he was in love with whatshername. He shook his head, wondering if he might have caught some rare and funky virus that made people temporarily go crazy. Temporarily, like for almost a year. What had he been thinking?

Well, to his defense, whatshername always played her part. She should have been an actress. Maybe she was. She'd lied to him about everything else, so why not her occupation too?

Listening to the dog scarf through his kibble, he knew this relationship was a good one. Not like old whatshername. He was over whatever strange mojo that made him think he'd found the perfect woman. From here on out, he was going to stick with dogs. It was safer on the heart.

Jake looked up, licked his jowls, belched once and gave a hopeful wag of his tail. Ethan chuckled. Safer on the heart, yes. It was manners Jake could stand to work on.

"Ready, boy? The park beckons."

~ * ~

Cassidy stirred, stretching lazily. She froze, breath held as a slight weight shifted next to her.

"Oh no, you don't belong up here." She tugged at the cover, trying to dislodge Tessa, who skillfully shifted, yet seemingly stayed in the same place, her dark eyes pleading silently.

"Look, I lugged all your stuff in and set you up a nice, comfy spot out in the utility room. You have everything in there you could want." It was impossible to believe they had even more stuff still at Cindy's place that needed to be brought over. She gave the blanket a harder tug, still not convincing Tessa to move.

"Scat, go." She looked around and spotted Remi lying at the foot of the bed, watching her, his tongue lolling. "I have an eight-thirty meeting and I need to make the bed. Now get off, you two." Tugging and yanking, she finally got the dogs down and the bed more or less acceptable. "Honestly." Fuming, she regarded her charges, hands resting on her hips. "Cindy spoiled you."

And if she was going to be a good substitute, she needed to spoil them a little too. After her meeting. Right now, she needed to clean up and go. She could grab breakfast on the way. She eyed the list on the table, under the glass paperweight, outlining their morning walk. They'd never know if she postponed it till later. They were dogs. Time meant nothing to them, right?

She could make her meeting, dash home for the park thing with them and then return to work. She'd have fulfilled her obligation for the day and everyone would be happy. Moments later, fresh from the shower and satisfied with her decision, she dressed and slipped her heels on. She'd already filled their bowls. She needed just a moment to gather her things. This was going to work out just fine. All she needed was to modify it slightly.

Dismay crashed into her like a wall as Tessa trotted up to her, tail aloft, a pink sparkly sweater in her mouth. Close behind stood Remi, a leash trailing from his mouth. On the floor already lay his denim vest.

"Oh brother." She eyed the eager anticipation on their faces and the trail of clothing and leashes. Apparently, they understood time a little better than she had given them credit for. Sighing, caving in, she reached for Tessa's sparkly sweater. "But what about my meeting?"

~ * ~

Jake pulled eagerly at his leash, his long tail whipping in the air as they neared the park entrance. Swinging the gate open just enough to allow them through, Ethan unhooked the leash, releasing Jake. With a bark, he was gone, racing to join his canine pals.

Looping the leash through his belt, Ethan stuffed his hands in the pockets of his jeans and studied the attendees. He offered a friendly wave to some of the doggie moms and dads that he knew. A few of the dogs came up, wagging around, begging a pat, before racing off again.

"Jake's looking good."

Ethan spun around at the feminine purr behind him, feeling himself go tense. "Yep, he loves these morning runs," he replied to the brunette standing almost eye to eye with him. He'd figured out pretty quick Gwen was hot into him weeks ago. The fact that she came to this park, when there were others closer to her, was a good indicator. She never brought a dog, so he surmised she just came to prowl around, sniffing for available males. And it seemed he was pretty high up on her list of desirable ones. So far, he'd been unsuccessful in convincing her he didn't return the favor. He wasn't into needy lionesses on the hunt. She had a way of making him feel like a chunk of raw meat.

She inched closer, enough for him to breathe in her almost overpowering perfume. Some floral stuff mixed with more flowers. Sort of like walking into a funeral parlor full of sympathy bouquets. Her ample bosom brushed his sleeve and he inched further back.

"And what about you, Ethan? What do you love in the morning?"

He could imagine what she wanted to hear, and he wasn't about to encourage her. He rocked back another step. "Coffee," he replied instead. "Bacon and eggs. Pancakes."

Her hopeful smile slowly faded. Whatever she might have said back was lost when he heard a cry of frustration and a gleeful bark. Whirling, he looked for the source of the sounds.

"Remi! Stop that!"

He recognized the little brown and white ticked dog racing freely now that his leash was dropped. Or pulled from the hand of the woman in bright red heels. Heels? At a dog park? Her black business suit and red hat looked equally out of place. And didn't she know you were supposed to take their leashes off inside the fence? Apparently not, because the other little dog was still attached to her leash as well, wrapped around the woman's wrist. Now that her partner was free, the little blond and white dog spun in circles, mad to join him. In her hand, the hapless woman clutched a cell phone, wedged up near her ear.

Rocking back on his heels, he took in the show, smothering a smile. Remi, full of freedom, darted just far enough to stay out of reach but close enough to keep the woman in pursuit. The woman, a pretty, petite brunette with a serious up do topped by a rolled brim chenille hat, stumbled along in her heels and all but dragging the scruffy Chi/terrier along. She alternated between hissing at Remi through clenched teeth then pushing the phone back to her ear to talk rapidly to someone.

Seeing she wasn't making much ground, Ethan settled himself on a bench to watch, arms spread out comfortably. Gwen faded away like a ghostly specter. He remembered Remi, a Parsons Russell terrier and Australian Shepherd mixture, as being a handful on the best of days. The smaller one, a terrier/ Chihuahua and question mark, always struck him as a cute, well behaved pooch. Except, he'd never seen the pair here with the brunette. He'd definitely remember her.

"Remi!" She whispered fiercely to the little dog, who was having a delightful time, barking over his shoulder at her. She pressed the phone back up. "No, Adam, I agree we have to stay on schedule with this project. Any delay now could be disastrous. Tessa, come on! Yes, I have a meeting tomorrow with Mr. King and I should have some solid answers then." She lowered the phone, eyes cutting into the dog. "Remi!" She slapped the phone back to her ear. "What? No, everything's just fine, why do you ask? Where am I? Oh, out enjoying one of the offerings of our fine community. It's such a pleasant morning, I thought why not, right?" She offered a strained chuckle.

It was all Ethan could do to hold back his laughter. Clearly, she was trying to hold a meeting of some sort. Didn't she know a park, full of barking dogs and yelling people was the last place for that?

Finally, she hung up the call, tripping over Tessa's leash. Checking on Jake, Ethan climbed to his feet. He'd have to save these dogs from this woman or this woman from herself, he wasn't sure which.

Chapter Three

Cassidy was going to kill Remi. Things were going pretty good, all things considered, for her impromptu meeting. Or they were, until the little heathen yanked the leash from her hand. Heels, so perfect for the office and sidewalks, sank in the soft grass of the park. It had taken a degree in rocket engineering just to figure out how to get their cute sweater and jacket on in the first place. The extra time spent dressing them set her so far back, she had no choice but to dial in for the meeting from the park. She was thankful no one asked what the hullabaloo in the background was, though there was no mistaking the questions in Adam's voice.

Wondering how she was going to murder Remi, once she finally caught him, she was stunned to see the little wretch happily gallop over to a man kneeling in the dirt. A cute man. Laughing, he scooped Remi up in his arms, dodging disgusting facial licks. Her heart skipped a few beats as he approached her, holding Remi squiggling to his chest.

"He must be yours," he said, stopping before her, his ocean blue eyes stealing her breath.

"No. I mean, yes, he is. Now. He is. They are." Hearing the gibberish pouring from her mouth, she stopped, heat fanning her cheeks. Clearing her throat, she tried again. "They were my sister's dogs. I just inherited them. Yesterday."

He unhooked Remi's leash and set the wooly beast down again.

"I thought I recognized them."

"Why did you do that?" she asked in dismay, noticing Remi once more darted happily out of her reach. Without a leash trailing, she'd have no earthly hope to catch him.

He gave her a quizzical look, one that made her wonder what he was thinking. If it were possible, he looked even cuter with his head tilted a little to the side. Her chest thumped. He knelt again, reaching for Tessa and unhooking her leash. He gave her a friendly pat on the head and gentle push. Soon, she was off racing after Remi. Standing back up again, he gave her another quizzical look. "It's a dog park. They're supposed to run free and play."

Somehow, in all of Cindy's very detailed instructions, she had omitted that small detail.

He fingered the leash swinging from his belt loop, drawing her eyes to how his faded jeans molded to his fit body. "My dog is over there." He pointed to where four big dogs piled on each other in a fight. She easily heard the growls and barks over the rest of the park din. "The husky and shepherd mixed guy, kind of brown and gray with the black face and ears."

"He's fighting," she exclaimed, once she identified his dog on top of the pile, shocked he was so nonchalant about his dog's aggression.

"He's playing," he mildly corrected. "Jake knows those dogs. They're all buddies. In a moment or two they'll be chasing each other like first grade kids at recess."

"Jake?"

"My dog." He stuck his hand out. "I'm Ethan Sheppard."

"Cassidy Grant."

He smiled, the corners of his eyes crinkling. His hand was warm. She felt a spark jump from him to her, racing through her palm and into her arm.

"So, Cassidy, I take it you've never been to a dog park before."

She shook her head, torn between watching his to-die-for blue eyes, Remi and Tessa or the pack of fighting dogs now tearing off to another corner like marathon runners, barking. "Only when I need to go someplace to run around and bite people on the shins."

He laughed, a musical sound that made Cassidy smile despite herself. "No, seriously, my sister brought her dogs here all the time and it's part of the conditions of my inheritance with them. As are their silly outfits." Again, she shook her head. "Cindy didn't have children, so these two were her kids."

"Sorry."

"Me too." His condolence stabbed her in the heart, reminding her Cindy really was gone. Shaking the fact aside, she concentrated on his midnight hair that was thick and straight. How would it feel to touch those ringlets and waves? And what about her current predicament with the dogs. "So what do I do now?"

He blinked. "About what?"

"Getting those two back again. I can't stay here all day with them."

"Easy. When you're ready to go, just call them. Like this." He ripped out a whistle, sharp and shrill. Multiple heads turned their direction as dogs everywhere, and people, stopped to look. "Jake!" he called, patting his leg.

Within moments his dog galloped up, tongue lolling. At Ethan's extended stop sign palm, he slid to a stop on his haunches directly in front of them, dirt flying. Ethan reached out to pat his head. "Good boy, Jake." He turned back to Cassidy, a smile on his face. "Just like that. I assume they're obedience trained?"

Eyeing the monster-sized dog, she swallowed. "Yes. Probably. I think so." At least she hoped so.

"Cassidy Grant, meet Jake." He knelt at the bohemian beast's side, and whispered in his ear. Jake, still seated, politely offered her a paw. Taken aback, she hesitated before gingerly touching the foot. It was almost as large as a dessert plate.

"Okay, buddy, good job. Go play." Whirling, Jake bounded away, barking to his friends. Ethan stood back up, a grin on his face. "That's the newest thing he's learned."

Drawn into his mesmerizing blue eyes, the color of the ocean depths, she couldn't help but ask, "How long have you had him?"

"Four months."

He had a bit more experience over her at dog ownership. While she doubted she'd have Remi or Tessa shaking hands in four months, unless they already did and she didn't know it, she at least hoped they would come when she called them.

~ * ~

Cassidy sailed into the office an hour later. She'd patted her leg for at least fifteen minutes before the dogs stopped sniffing and barking and finally returned to her. Snapping their leashes on, and threating to never bring them back, she finally got them home. In route back, she discovered muddy paw prints all over her shoes and panty hose. How and when had she gotten muddy paws on her? That took another five minutes to change into another coordinating set and then catch the bus to the office.

"Cassidy! Have you seen this morning's paper?" Adam Gaines, her boss, caught her as she breezed to her desk.

"No, not yet. Why?" She dropped her bag under the desk and spun to face him, instantly knowing the news was not good. "*Punch* again?" That cartoonist was going to be the death of her. She held her hand out for *The Midland Gazette*.

Sure enough. On page four, neatly centered, was yet another cartoon aimed at I. R. King, the mayor of Midland. Didn't this Salty Kidd person have anything better to do than poke fun at the city leaders?

"King's going to blow a gasket when he sees that," Adam prophesized.

She handed the paper back. "He should be used to them by now. The Salty Kidd is harmless." And incredibly bored no doubt, whoever he or she was. "I'll smooth it over tomorrow should he say anything."

"I want you to find out who it is."

Her jaw dropped. "Adam, I can't. This person is clearly hiding their true identity with this silly name. There is also the Freedom of Speech thing to consider. The editor or publisher at the paper won't share who is behind the alias. And admittedly, this stupid little *Punch* strip is popular." Even if most of the targets seemed to be city officials and government leaders. While the artist preferred local targets, it wasn't unusual to find the occasional cartoons picturing higher elected officials like Congress or the President. She'd have to guess this person felt comfortable in their anonymity.

Adam sighed, tossing the paper back on Cassidy's desk. "You have charm and connections. You can find out who it is and suggest they find a new direction to throw their little cartoonish darts. It's an election year coming up. These stupid little popular strips could hurt King's chances at reelection."

"Adam, I—"

"If all else fails, Cassidy, resort to bribery if your charm doesn't work." With that, he spun and walked away.

~ * ~

Returning home with Jake from the park, Ethan tossed Jake a thick bone, the kind guaranteed to keep him occupied for hours, and pulled his bike away from the wall. Dodging lumbering buses, strollers and umbrellas, and potholes the size of moon craters, he considered himself lucky to reach work unscathed. Who carried umbrellas when there was a zero chance for rain?

He chained his bike, slung his backpack over his shoulder and jogged up the steps of the *Gazette*. Mitch met him at the top, lounging against the wall and sipping his normal expresso. Ethan halted, smelling the coffee from a foot away.

"Hey, pal, what's up?" Mitch greeted between swallows. "Have you heard the latest?"

"About?"

"I. R. King, of course."

The esteemed mayor of Midland, and Ethan's favorite political target. Of course with a name like that, how could he not be expected to poke fun once in a while? He wouldn't be doing his job otherwise. Actually, some time ago he'd unearthed the fact that his initials stood for Igor Randolph. Considering his background, the Igor probably came as a nod to the famous music composer, but he preferred to stick with the Frankenstein monstrous connotation instead. It was more fun. If the guy insisted on making himself an easier bulls-eye by using the letters, he'd happily go along with it.

"If I. R. King and those guys up on Ruler Hill would actually do something about the condition of this town, like fix our sidewalks for starters, they could probably push the Salty Kidd into an early retirement."

Mitch smirked, opening the door. "Then what would you do?"

Ethan shrugged. "Be forced to find a real job, I guess." Or have more time to see what happened with the woman who inherited the two little dogs. He'd tried to forget about her since leaving the park, but even Mitch's comments weren't good enough to fully distract him. Mitch and he grabbed the elevator. "So what did ole' I. R. do this time?"

"He's trying to take away the Love Locks."

Ethan's breath hitched and he took in Mitch's expression. "Seriously? What harm could they possibly cause the old sour puss?"

Mitch shrugged and they entered their shared office. Mitch dropped into his chair, leaning back and lacing his hands behind his head.

"How do you know for sure?" Ethan remained standing, propped next to his desk.

Mitch arched an eyebrow at his pal. "Kidding? Right?"

No, not really. Mitch was the paper's voice for political news and Ethan was the political cartoonist. They were a natural pair. Mitch wrote editorials and Ethan made fun of the facts. Mitch made the meetings on Ruler Hill. If folks discovered he was really the person behind the Salty Kidd, they would probably tar and feather him.

Dropping into his own chair, swiveling back, he considered the padlocks people placed around town, on gates, bridges and fences, to illustrate their love for one another. They painted names and initials on the padlocks and sometimes attached special mementos. They were a unified show of hopeful and lasting love, illustrated city wide. Despite his personal feelings on love now, since whatshername came into and then left his life, he still liked what the locks represented. And I. R. King hated them. Figures.

Chapter Four

Cassidy finally reached her front door, grateful to be home. For whatever reason, her day had been especially demanding. Normally she thrilled at the pressure and challenge of a typical day at the office. Today she just wanted to crash on the sofa, watch reruns of whatever was popular last season and binge on ice cream. Chocolate, peanut butter and fudge. With lots of whipped cream. And cherries.

Maybe the fact that Cindy really was gone had finally hit her.

Swinging the door open, inhaling the vanilla reed infuser scent, she stopped dead in her tracks. Tessa and Remi stood, tails wagging, leashes trailing and sweaters placed before them.

"Are you kidding me?" She dropped her laptop and purse, wincing as the laptop thudded. "You already went out." *Except that was this morning.* "Okay, fine, whatever. But this is going to be a fast trip. You understand me?"

She hooked up the leashes, pushing their clothing out of the way. "I am not up to trying to figure that stuff out again. Thousands of dogs have no coats to wear, you two will do just fine for a short walk." Snatching up her purse again, she trailed them out the door. Maybe that good looking guy would be there again. Ethan. The image of his midnight hair and deep ocean blue eyes swam before her, taking her breath.

Ethan had been stealing her thoughts most the day, causing her to drift off during meetings and conference calls. He really wasn't her type, she tried to tell herself. He was too…natural. Not refined enough. He was too…rough. He wasn't polished enough. He showed up in public with his shirt tail hanging out, for Pete's sake. The man had no self-pride.

By the time they reached the park, she'd convinced herself he wasn't worth thinking about again. Except she couldn't help but do a fast check around and didn't see either him or his oversized dog. Disappointment splashed over her, surprising her. Bending to unhook Tessa and Remi's leashes, she snapped her fingers at them first.

"You two had better come to me the very first time I hit my leg. No messing around. Got it?"

Watching them streak off, barking and leaping, she crossed her arms over her chest. Despite the long and detailed list of instructions, she really was clueless what to do with them. They seemed more in control of their lives right now. Wasn't she the one who was supposed to be the leader? Maybe Ethan could help her out, just until she figured out her new role with them.

He seemed very good with dogs. If she happened to run into him here again, she could ask. Offer it as a professional service. She could even pay him for his assistance. That felt better. It sounded better too.

She watched Remi chase the other dogs, much larger than himself, barking and running between their legs. Tessa followed, keeping a safer distance away. Settling onto a bench, she felt a tear slipping down her cheek. She wiped it away. These were Cindy's babies. How many hours had she spent here, laughing at every insane thing they did and thinking it was adorably cute? Did she ever wish even one of her sisters would come and share it with her?

"Cindy, I really wish you were here now," she whispered, heaving a breath.

The clanging ring of the food vendors at their carts drove her to her feet. Stomach growling, she reached in her purse for some bills. Vendor cart food was not normally something she enjoyed, but right now, she was desperate and hungry. Plus she kind of doubted the furry beasts would come when she slapped her leg. At least not for the first dozen times.

Purchasing a burger with the works, with fries and a soda, and a plain hot dog with no bun, she returned to the bench. The burger was overcooked, but acceptable, slathered in an assortment of toppings. The fries were slightly undercooked but warm, so she enjoyed them, slowly munching as she watched the dogs endlessly romp. Didn't they ever get tired?

Okay, she could see where bringing them to the park was good, since they doubtlessly would have worn the tread off her floor by now.

Finally, as the sun started sinking and coolness nipped the air, she grabbed the plain hot dog, stood and slapped her leg, calling the dogs to her.

"Tessa! Remi! Look what I have." She waved the hot dog invitingly, thrilling when they started back her direction. Snapping the leashes on, Remi first of course, she offered them small bites of hot dog. "Good dogs. Here's a reward for coming without a fuss."

Hot dog gone and pets safely leashed, it was time to return home.

David was waiting for her, sitting patiently in his truck, jamming out to some song. Remi and Tessa surged forward in a happy welcome.

"David, hi. Where's Karen?" And what about Karen's allergies? She looked around.

"Just me today," he explained, bending to pet the dogs. He scooped Remi up and held the dog upside down. Remi wiggled happily, still trying to lick David's face. "Karen sent me over with their stuff." He slashed her a wicked grin. "You took them out not being properly dressed? For shame."

She sent her brother-in-law a scowl. "Don't push it. They survived and had a wonderful time. How much more stuff do they have?" She craned her neck, trying to look through the tinted windows of his truck. And where was she going to put it all?

"Almost as much stuff as our kids have. Here." David replied, depositing Remi and handing over two small boxes. "Karen went over earlier today and got it all packed up. She also added some of Cindy's stuff for you too."

She wasn't sure she was ready for her sister's possessions yet. Just having the dogs was hard enough. Balancing the boxes in the crook of her arm, she led David inside, greeted the doorman and dropped the leashes once they were safely inside the apartment. The dogs scampered off around the corner and soon the sounds of slurping water flowed out to Cassidy and David.

"Gee, don't you ever let those poor babies drink?"

She stomped her foot on his toes as she reached for the top of the stack of boxes he carried. "Put the rest in the living room." She followed him, setting the boxes down along with the last ones she still hadn't unpacked yet.

Remi trotted happily into the room, holding something in his mouth. Tail wagging, he offered it to David, barking once.

"Oh no. That's one of my best shoes," Cassidy cried in dismay. She took the shoe from David and shook it at Remi. "Bad dog! My stuff! You leave it alone." Turning it over, she fingered the damage.

"Easy, Cassidy. He's just grieving."

"He's got a wagon load of toys and bones to chew up and grieve with," she shot back, tossing the shoe aside.

David spread his hands out. "Hey, I'm just saying you're all grieving. Karen, you, and them."

"Is Karen chewing up your best shoes too?"

"No, but I think it might be easier on me if she did. Consider yourself lucky it's only a shoe."

"I'll trade you."

~ * ~

Ethan awoke before Jake stirred. Moving his arm down to pet Jake's ears, he crawled up, trying to snuggle under Ethan's t-shirt. He pushed the mutt aside with a chuckle.

"Jake, you big mug, you won't fit under there. Hate to tell ya, bud, but you're no puppy. Despite how you act sometimes." He grabbed the dog's ears with both hands and tugged playfully. "Wanna go to the park, buddy? See if Remi and Tessa dragged their new mommy there again?"

The doorbell rang and Jake's head shot up, brows furrowed. Ethan chuckled, shoving the dog out of his way. "Some protector you are." Who could be at his door at such an early hour? It was just past seven.

He scratched his belly and crossed to the door, halting in mid yawn as he swung it open. Then silently cursed himself.

"Good morning, sleepyhead." Gwen beamed brightly. She lifted up two carry out cups of coffee, heavy aroma steaming into the room. "You

19

did say you liked coffee."

Stunned, he took a step back, keeping a firm hold on the door. He didn't think she'd try pushing in, but this was Gwen. Anything was possible. What the heck was she doing in his neighborhood? At seven in the morning? At his door? Dread swirled around him as strong as the lifting scent of coffee.

She waved one cup at him expectantly. Jake nosed in and he quickly motioned the dog back and into a sit.

"Uh, look, this wasn't necessary." Especially at the crack of dawn. "I can manage my own coffee."

"Of course you can, silly boy. This is just a friendly gesture."

Except they weren't friends. Nor did he want to be friends. And he personally hated the term silly boy. Her eager smile sent cold chills pouring over him worse than the coldest shower he'd ever taken. He started to close the door, trying to block both her and the scents of coffee and overpowering flowers.

"Thank you but I can't accept this. You don't have to bring me anything. Good bye."

He shut the door, taking a moment to turn the lock. He swung a look around, ensuring all curtains were pulled closed too. Just in case she tried gawking in or rapping at the glass. Finally, he stood, arms crossed, and glared at Jake. "Some protection you are, buddy. Would you help a thief carry out the goods too?"

Moments later, watching Jake bury his nose in the bowl, he leaned on the counter, cradling a fresh cup of coffee. Thoughts of Miss All Business Cassidy filled his mind and erased memories of Gwen's unexpected visit. Images of Cassidy had stayed on his mind while he was working yesterday, trying to drum up some catchy images of I.R. King and his dislike for the town's Love Locks. Sharing a dinner with Jake afterward, she flittered through his thoughts and finally kept his dreams company as he slept. Which was probably why he beat Jake awake.

She was something, he couldn't quite put his finger on. She didn't strike him as a dog person, so he admired her taking on two of them. How had her sister died? Were they close? He remembered Remi and Tessa's mom bringing them to the park. He didn't know her name, but she was quiet and kept to herself mostly, except for a few friends she sometimes met there. They laughed at the dogs and the toddlers if some of her friends brought theirs. She never looked his way once that he knew of and his chick magnet was usually working overtime whenever he was in public places like the park. Even when he was busy watching Jake or hanging with any of his friends who showed up.

How he ended up attracting a hunting lioness like Gwen was beyond him. He barely remembered noticing her till she landed in his face like a wrecking ball.

Cassidy Grant seemed different from how he remembered her sister. She caught your eye, whether she knew it or not. She was a hard woman to miss. Easy on the eyes, despite the fact she had no clue to how to dress for a dog park. What did she do for a living? Something that required dressing as a business exec and holding phone calls in public. He had thought he would get high on her perfume yesterday. It wasn't strong florals like some women wore, but a subtle hint mixed with warm tones of woods and spices. Whatever it was, he wanted to smell it all day long. He wouldn't mind bathing in it

He chuckled. Jake belched, then licked his chops, gazing expectantly at Ethan, his tail beating a tattoo on the floor.

"Sorry, bud. Ready?" He grabbed up the leash and his coffee mug.

Rounding the corner of the dog area, he caught himself searching for Cassidy. Or Remi and Tessa, as he figured they were probably going to be the easiest to spot. He released Jake and spun around in a circle, looking for the face wearing a red hat that so filled his thoughts and dreams.

Chapter Five

Armed with a cold hot dog she bribed from the vendor, she released the dogs. "Another hot dog will be yours if you come back when I call you," she promised. Stuffing their leashes in her purse, she watched them streak off, Remi in the lead naturally. She looked around but did not see Ethan or the monstrous Jake. Heading to a bench, she heard a shout. Too late, she swiveled as a tennis ball slammed into her shoulder.

"Ouch!" Grabbing at her shoulder, she froze, pain ricocheting down her arm. The yellow ball, full of slobber and dirt, bounced on the ground and rolled along the grass.

"Gosh, Lady, I sure am sorry about that." A teen-aged boy with overly long hair flowing from under a blue cap raced up to her, followed by a hairy retriever who scooped up the ball, along with three others already in its mouth. Cassidy eyed the dog, thinking it looked like an oversized chipmunk, before turning her gaze back to the kid holding the ball launcher.

"I swear I didn't see you," he continued. "Are you okay?"

"Yes, I think so." The pain was subsiding now, but doubtlessly the weapon left an imprint of hair and slobber. On the blazer she planned to wear to her meeting with Mayor King.

"Great. Sorry." Flashing her a smile, the teen-age kid snapped his fingers at the chipmunk dog and they both raced away, their long hair flowing.

"Bet that leaves a bruise."

The deep voice made Cassidy spin around, so fast that the park kept spinning. Latching her eyes on Ethan, her heart skipped a few beats. "It

22

might," she agreed, suddenly breathless. She smelled coffee on his breath and noticed the travel thermos hooked to his belt loop. Along with a leather dog leash.

"I was hoping to see you here."

"You were?" Surprise rolled over Cassidy as she balanced herself alongside a tree. "Why?"

Ethan grinned. "I don't really know." He gave a shrug.

She rubbed her shoulder, still stinging from the assault. "Actually, I had wanted to see you. I… I have a business proposition for you."

He brightened for a fleeting second, then stuffed his hands in his pockets. "What kind of proposition?"

"Well, you seem so good with the dogs. I've never had any experience with them. I was wondering if I could hire your services. Your expertise. To teach me about how to handle these two."

Despite not one word she said coming out sounding like a question, she waited, breath held, for his reaction. He arched one dark eyebrow at her, paused to look around the park and settle back to her. He rocked back on his heels, a slow smile creeping over his face.

"You want to hire me to teach you about dogs?"

"Yes." She nodded. "I would pay you for your time of course."

"There are obedience lessons offered around town."

Cassidy pulled in a breath. Was he turning her down? "Yes, I know that. I mean I assume that." She rethought the offer. "I don't think it's so much they need obedience." David swore they didn't. "It's more I need dog knowledge." True enough. Other than Remi's destruction of her shoe, and a few minor things, they were good little house guests. "I need to know how to bond with them. Like Cindy had."

He gave a slow nod. "Tell you what, Miss Grant, why don't we go to Perks and we can discuss this more in depth? My treat."

She pictured the double decker red bus now permanently installed as a coffee house and popular gathering place. She had not been there but had always meant to. "What about the dogs?"

He shook his head. "Not a problem. They have outside tables complete with doggie hook ups. Now, how do you like your coffee?"

Using her cold hot dog, she bribed Remi and Tessa to come. As she snapped their leashes on, she was acutely aware of Ethan's quiet study. Naturally his dog came with one call, sliding to a stop like a baseball player stealing home base, and waiting patiently for the leash with no bribery needed. It irked Cassidy, but also reinforced that Ethan would be a good choice for this business arrangement. If he could show her how to get her dogs to respond half as well as his did, it was worth any price. And to have them sleep on their beds instead of hers and not chew her things. A little less barking would be nice too. While she was working on her mental wish list, would having them pick up their own toys and things be asking too much?

~ * ~

Walking alongside each other, they passed over a bridge. Hooked on the railing were dozens of padlocks. A sigh built up in Ethan as he leaned over to examine a few. Most had initials or names scratched into the metal. How could King possibly have an issue with these?

"Something wrong?"

Ethan's head swung back up. She stood, hand on her hip, watching him curiously. "No. Just thinking about…" His thought trailed off.

"They bother some people." Cassidy nodded her head at the locks.

"I can't see how. They're harmless."

"They might be considered one step away from vandalism or graffiti. They contribute to the destruction of city property."

He snorted, adding a frown for good measure. He fingered a couple locks, tugging at them. "They also symbolize human beings' emotions for one another. It's a public show of their commitment to each other."

A slow smile crept over Cassidy's face. "You sound like a hopeless romantic."

Ethan gave a shake of his head. "Not anymore. I just don't think anyone has the right to stomp on those who do find love and want to tell the world about it. Or at least tell the town of Midland."

~ * ~

They reached Perks. Cassidy sat with the dogs, tethered to the table, while Ethan went inside to buy their drinks. Returning, he handed hers

24

over and straddled the bench, dropping a biscuit to each of the dogs.

"So tell me about this suggestion of yours?"

Cassidy glanced around the immediate area. A couple of other patrons also had their dogs with them. Like Jake, their dogs all lay quietly at their side. Unlike Remi, who once he finished the biscuit, began lunging to the end of his leash, sniffing and woofing. Cassidy swallowed back her embarrassment. How had Cindy done this?

She brushed the top of the table off as Ethan took a sip of his coffee. Business deal, she reminded herself. Think of this as any other business deal. "Well, clearly I am new to this dog ownership thing. And I am impressed with how well Jake obeys you." She paused, watching the slow smile spread over his face, crinkling his eyes. A shot of something warm stole over her.

"I was thinking it would be a good match for you to help me with these two, especially Remi." She looked down and gave a little tug on his leash, reining him closer. "And I would pay you of course."

"I see. And what exactly did you want help with?"

"Remi chewed up one of my best shoes last night. David said he was just grieving, but I can't have him chewing up my closet. They both insist on sleeping in my bed, despite all the fine things they have. You wouldn't believe all the stuff they have."

He chuckled.

"I have to use bribery to get them to come back to me."

"Yes, I did notice that hot dog trick. It was successful. However, I might not be the best person to help you. Jake sleeps with me."

She fought back the automatic cringe. It was a personal preference, she told herself. Surely he could train his dog to stay off the bed if he wanted to. Right? Surely he could show her how?

Her gaze traveled to his naked left hand, curled around the mug. Above them, on top the open deck, a small group of people erupted into cheers over something.

"Your girlfriend doesn't mind sharing the bed with a dog?" The question popped out of her mouth like cinnamon rolls from a tube. Instantly fresh warmth spread over her, like stepping into an oven. What made her ask that?

A variety of expressions passed over Ethan's face. "I don't have one," he said finally, his voice low. "Guess you could say it wasn't a good choice."

What could that mean? Interest filled her mind. "Well, that makes it easy I suppose. Now, what do you think about us working together?" Why did it seem like she was suddenly incoherent? Opting for saying less, she waited, her breath caught, and chest pounding. She could drown in those eyes.

Suddenly his lips parted and her pulse skipped forward. He cut her a grin and extended his hand.

"Okay, Cassidy, you have a deal. We can give it a try. Shall we start Saturday?"

"Saturday is fine. Nine o' clock?" At his nod, she wrote out her address and directions on a napkin emblazed with Perks and a double decker bus emblem.

Chapter Six

"Wow, you're sure in a great mood. What happened?" Dana asked. "You're like humming and everything."

Cassidy studied her friend, Dana, and took the files she held out. Had she really been humming? Curious. She smiled, glancing around the office. "I met someone. At the dog park. He's going to help me with controlling the dogs."

"Why are you whispering?"

Was she? Clearly, she was getting addled minded. "I don't know. Oh, Dana, he's so cute!"

Dana squealed, dropping into a chair and crossing her legs. She grabbed Cassidy's arm. "Tell me everything."

Excitement bubbling up, Cassidy started from their first meeting, ending with their discussion at Perks less than an hour before. "All I can say is, Saturday can't get here soon enough," she concluded.

Dana gave her a dreamy smile. "Beyond dogs, what else do you hope he does?"

Cassidy shook her head, about to deny any further interest.

"This is me asking, girlfriend," Dana reminded her.

Those ocean blue eyes and soft smile. She could stand to see a lot more of that. Could they maybe move beyond just dealing with the dogs? The racing of her heart dared her to deny the wish.

"Okay, deal breaker time, Cass. What could he do to turn off that dreamy look on your face?"

Was she wearing a dreamy look? Oh, probably. "Okay." She sighed, shifting her weight. "Talking endlessly about his ex, definitely a sign

27

he's not over her." Which he hadn't. He barely mentioned his past relationship, just it being a bad choice. And she brought it up first. Fair enough. "Making me do all the leg work for a date, like he never leaves his apartment." Instead, he initiated the trip to Perks. Okay, so far, so good. He was over his past relationship and he got out once in a while.

Dana studied her. "No unsolicited serenading?"

She shook her head.

"Pretending to be a Renaissance man by throwing around those ridiculous M'lady phrases?"

"No." He didn't seem the type to even know about Renaissance fairs. Except his opinion of the Love Locks and his comment about openly showing love knocked at her heart. She'd always been a sucker for tenderness in a man.

"Endlessly talking of his mommy or best bro threesome? Treating the get-together like a therapy session?"

"No to both."

Dana squeezed her arm, beaming. "He sounds like he's off to a good start, Cass. Give him a chance. Kelly and I were going to ask you to join us this weekend, but I'll tell her you've got other plans. We can all go to Eddie's party next week."

"Dana, you and Kelly are the best."

Dana smiled. "Of course we are. Now take those files and get going, or you'll be late for your meeting."

"Meeting! Oh, my word! I forgot all about it." Leaping forward, Cassidy clutched the folders. "I. R. will be livid." Dashing down the hall, she heard Dana's hearty chuckle and parting call.

"You're welcome."

Cassidy slid into her chair, keenly aware of I. R. King's solemn stare and the surprised glances from the other board members. I. R. had been some high-ranking officer in the military in his prime and now he expected his meetings to run with that same precision. To him, tardiness was as bad a crime as treason or going AWOL.

"As I was saying," I. R. continued dryly, "the cyclists are taking over the city. Why just the other day I nearly ran one of them over when he turned straight into my car."

"We did install the wider sidewalks, to encourage they ride there instead of the auto lanes."

I. R. slapped his fist on the table, the sound reverberating. Water rippled in the drinking glasses. "Precisely! We encouraged them and now there are so many, they no longer fit on the sidewalks. They are taking over the rest of the city. They're like feeding pigeons in the park. It starts with a few innocent ones and before you know it, you have inadvertently encouraged countless numbers." His gaze lingered on the man who spoke a moment prior, then came to rest on Cassidy. "We need to decide what can be done about this, and still remain within the lines of politically correctness."

Cassidy bit back a sigh. With I. R., it was always what was politically correct. He'd never sully his hands to do something underhanded or politically unappealing. So why did that cartoonist, the Salty Kidd, seem to dislike him so much? And how was she supposed to find out who that person really was?

~ * ~

Who was David? The question burned in Ethan's brain for hours. Her boyfriend? She'd asked if he had a girlfriend, so it stood to reason she might have a male companion. Already he found himself rankling, slightly defensive against this unknown person.

Ethan tossed down his pencil. It could be her brother, for crying out loud. It could be the neighbor next door. David could be anyone. He could be…her boyfriend. If so, he was as clueless about dogs as Cassidy was, except he knew enough to recognize they too grieved. Which was something he suspected Cassidy hadn't considered.

Ethan blew out a breath. He had his work cut out for him. And more than just the dogs. Cassidy was affecting him in ways not even old whatshername had been able to. He couldn't get her out of his mind, and couldn't wait for Saturday to arrive, nine am.

Would David be there?

"Is tossing pencils down the hot new way to draw?" Mitch asked, strolling into their office and dropping into his chair with a thud and a creak. He eyed the pile of pencils littering Ethan's desk. "Can't find the sharpener?"

"No, just not happy with what I've got."

Mitch leaned over and studied the nearly blank page before Ethan. "Yeah, I can see why. So who is David?"

Ethan's head shot up, eyes wide, then followed Mitch's gaze to the name scrolled in the corner. Had he really written the guy's name? Heat fanned his cheeks under Mitch's amused stare.

"Remember the girl I told you about? At the park? Well, today we went to Perks and she mentioned David."

Mitch shrugged. "Okay, so who is he?"

"He told Cassidy one of the dogs chewed up her shoe because he was grieving."

"And?"

Ethan gathered his pencils, carefully placing them back in their proper trays. "And what? That's all I know."

"You think he's your competition?"

Ethan scowled. "Look, I'm helping her with her sister's dogs. David, whoever he is, doesn't seem able to do that. So no, wise guy, I don't think he's my competition." He snatched up an eraser and attacked the name on the strip.

Mitch leaned back, hands laced behind his back. "You know, it would be so much easier if they would just tell us what they want. We're not psychics and yet they expect us to read their minds." He snorted in derision.

Ethan shot him a glance, but Mitch ignored it, continuing his tirade. "Like when we take them to a restaurant. Man, can we ever get it all right? If we're decent to the wait staff, does she think we're a nice guy or a push over? If we have a couple drinks, does she think we're a relaxed social drinker or an alcoholic? If we get a big meal, does she think we're hungry or just a pig?"

Ethan's hand stilled. He clutched the eraser. "Mitch, I'm not taking her to dinner. I'm helping her with the dogs. That's all." A niggling voice rose up, teasing him, hinting he'd like to take her to dinner. "Besides, how was I supposed to know whatshername didn't really mean it when she said she wanted to go to the Burger Hut? She said she liked the Two

Can Dine for $9.99 Deal."

Mitch shrugged.

"I thought she was just trying to be frugal, with the wedding coming up."

"You need to work on your mind reading skills. That may be what she said, but it wasn't what she meant."

Ethan lifted his hands into the air. 'Exactly! That is why I'm not taking Cassidy to dinner. Because I have no mind-reading powers. I couldn't even read your mind."

Mitch sighed and dropped his chair back. "Okay, fine. If you're not serious about this chick, I think we should register you for an online dating account. You know, get you back out there fishing again." He grinned, making a casting and reeling motion with his hands.

"Mitch," Ethan warned, realizing his co-worker was ignoring him by rifling through some papers.

"Yeah, here it is." He waved a computer print-out. "I saved this one just for you, buddy boy. 'Doting Dudes' is the name of the site. You set up an account, profile, and all that stuff. Girls check you out and send emails if they're interested."

Despite his misgivings, Ethan scanned the page as Mitch tossed it to him. "And how would I list myself?" he asked. "I'm not a divorced male."

"You're still single, buddy boy. You're engagement to whatshername doesn't count." He paused thoughtfully, rubbing his chin and breaking into a big grin. "However, I do have to say donating all that catered meal from the reception to the homeless shelter was classic, pal. Real classy."

Ethan shrugged, folding the paper. "I paid for it, she left. Seems like the best use for it." He sure hadn't wanted it. Taking aim, he sailed the paper airplane back to Mitch. "Keep this. I'm not ready for 'Doting Dudes' or any other online site." There was always Gwen if he wanted female companionship. Just the thought made a shiver crawl over him.

Mitch worked the folds out of the paper. "So you're going to waste your time on this dog park chick? Except you're not even going to date her. Man, I just don't understand you."

Ethan shrugged. He picked the eraser back up again, scrubbing a little more at the name on the page.

"So when you agreed to this… arrangement, did you shake hands?"

"Yes, we did, smarty. What's it to you?"

Mitch shrugged, a grin on his lips. "So you think she wanted more? Like a fast peck on the cheek? Or on the back of the hand? Come on, man, tell me you at least considered it."

Growling an oath, Ethan lobbed his eraser at Mitch's chest. He exited their office as Mitch's amused chuckle reached him.

~ * ~

"Miss Grant. Do you have a moment?" I. R.'s request stopped her just short of the door. She'd hoped to slip out with the rest of the attendees, and remain under his radar. Apparently not. Drawing in a breath, she clutched the files and notes to her chest and turned around. His stony expression made her feel like she was facing the firing squad.

She pasted on the brightest smile she could. "Mr. King? How can I help you?"

"Has Gaines said anything to you about that crazy cartoonist?"

She nodded. "He has," she hedged.

I. R. sank into his chair and steepled his fingers, staring at her. "That fool could ruin my chances at re-election. I want him or her stopped. Immediately."

"Mr. King, as I explained to Mr. Gaines, it really will be impossible to learn this person's identity. There are laws—"

"Miss Grant," I. R. waved his hand, halting her speech. "Perhaps you did not understand me." His cold eyes pinned her to the carpet. "I said, I want him or her stopped. Immediately."

Cassidy bit down on her cheek until she tasted blood. She squared her shoulders, meeting his stony glare without flinching. He was only the mayor, not the mighty ruler he wanted to be. Carefully, she lowered one hand to the table top, fingers splayed for balance as she selected her answer. Because she was only going to get one answer out.

"Mr. King. I understood you very well. You are perfectly clear. And I hope I am making myself just as clear when I say there are federal laws

32

designed to protect people's freedom of speech. That, Mr. King, is what this individual is exercising with that comic strip. Lots of artists have used this medium to give voice to the concerns of the common man." She paused, straightening back up. "If your chances of re-election are such a concern to you, Sir, perhaps you could take note of what the strip is really saying. Now, if you will excuse me."

Turning, she slowly marched from the room, not daring to take a breath till she was clear of his doorway. Feet wobbling, she finally reached her office. She pulled her desk drawer out and dug around for her bottle of aspirin. Hands shaking, she wrestled the cap off and shook out two, swallowing them with the bottle of leftover cold cappuccino.

Well, there was going to be a hefty price to pay once King talked to her boss. In the meantime, she still had calls to make and a job to do. After today, that might change.

She trailed her fingertip along the cappuccino bottle, her thoughts returning to Ethan. As much as she looked forward to Saturday, and his help, she wondered...she nibbled her bottom lip. He said he didn't have a girlfriend. So, did that mean...?

"Cassidy! What did you do, girl?"

She jumped as Kelly barreled breathlessly into her office. "I just heard the story. I can't believe you told old man King off. Are you crazy? Or just wondering what the unemployment line looks like?"

Cassidy tried to work up a grin at Kelly's sassy quip but failed. There was too much ring of truth to it. She shook her head. "No, I don't really know what got into me. I just reacted." Totally out of character for her. Maybe this was the human equivalent of chewing shoes. "I think I might be grieving."

Kelly patted her pile of frizz and studied her, slipping into a chair. She reached out, gripping Cassidy's arm. "Dana told me about the dog guy. That's so cool. But you know, there's no shame in saying you're missing your sister."

"Cassidy!"

The barking sound of her name ringing out made both Cassidy and Kelly jump. Kelly shot her a look before slinking from the room like a scolded schoolgirl. Cassidy rose, straightening her outfit and facing her boss.

"Yes, Adam?"

"Don't pretend you don't know what I'm here about," he said, shaking a finger at her. "King just came from my office. Any guesses what he had to say to me?"

She grit her teeth, hearing the clicking. If she ever found out who that Salty Kidd was, which would be incredible if she did, she was going to throttle him or her. Or at least break every pencil they owned.

"Adam, surely you can see the reasonable side to this."

"Doesn't matter. King wants this person found. Reasonable has no place in the picture. That is what you need to focus on."

Cassidy sighed and gripped the edge of her desk. She pulled in a breath. "Adam. I think I need to take a little time…off. I just lost my sister and…I think I need to grieve. Or something."

"Something?' Adam seemed momentarily taken aback. "You're not sure if you need to grieve or not?"

Was that her problem? "Grieve or chew up a shoe."

His startled expression made her look away, suddenly awkward. More proof she was addled. She was never awkward, until now.

Chapter Seven

Adam had not been thrilled about it, but he agreed to give Cassidy two days off. Well, a day and a half—what was left of Thursday and all of Friday. That would take her straight into Saturday when Ethan came over. An overwhelming sense of relief spilled over her as she packed her bag to leave work. She said good-bye to Kelly and Dana and stepped into the bright afternoon sunshine.

Purse swinging from her elbow, she strolled the streets. Today, she'd stop in and see Karen. Birds called overhead, reminding her of King's pigeon comment. Bicyclists and skateboarders buzzed around her, some following the traffic and others staying to the sidewalks. She paused at The Wish Wall. This was the latest community improvement project and it seemed to be doing well. It had started out on a construction privacy wall she happened to spot one day. She ran the suggestion to Adam and the city council and everyone liked the idea. Even I. R. King embraced it.

Soon permanent, stronger versions were strategically installed around the city. Walls, each measuring five feet high, stretched for several feet in key locations. Chalk and paints were provided in small cubbyhole cabinets. People filled in the blank behind leading questions like "I wish—" or "Before I die, I want to—"

Cassidy loved to stop at various locations and read the newest additions to the walls. Reponses ranged from short term to far reaching, from romantic to daring. Some were profound, several were silly and many were heart wrenching sad. She tried to imagine the faces that went along with the wishes.

I wish to go to college. I wish I could travel the world. I wish Sami Baker knew I loved her. I wish my grandma didn't have to die. I wish my mom and dad would get back together. I wish I could go up in a hot air balloon. I wish my brother would come home. I wish I could make better grades. I wish for peace. I wish to pass my chemistry test tomorrow.

Before I die, I want to kiss Bobby Thompson. Before I die, I want to sail around the globe. Before I die, I want to tell all my children how much I love them one more time. Before I die, I want to live.

Some made her cry while others made her laugh. What had started as a chance observation while passing a construction site turned into a positive step for the city. She'd never asked her sisters if they read the walls. Were there wishes from Karen or Cindy scribbled somewhere on one of the walls? Swallowing, she imaged the person who wanted to live before they died. Her chest burned, low and sharp. Was it someone old or young? Did they face their imminent death as they wrote the words? Or where they simply being realistic? What had Cindy wanted and never said?

Remembering the weekend at Rainbow Beach, she brushed a fast forming tear away. If only they knew how little time they had left when they were there. She glanced around, then reached for a chalk. Blue, because it was a pretty color. Pulling in her bottom lip, she rested the stick against the cold metal of the wall, drawing in a breath.

I wish I had spent more time with my sister before she died.

Finished, she leaned back, staring at the words. In black and blue, they seemed almost shocking. The confession did nothing to ease her guilt. Well, she still had one more sister.

Karen was home, the television was blaring and the kids were screaming. Cassidy paused at the front door. "Is this a good time for a visit?"

"Sure, come on in." Karen waved her in while scooping up the toddler trying to make a break for the freedom beyond the door. "I'm just wrangling the wild posse. School is out today."

"Um, yes. Teacher in-service." Cassidy watched as Karen brushed aside some clothing and toys to clear her a chair.

"I never really understood what those were for. Some legal way to torture us parents?" Karen commented, sitting and holding the toddler to her shoulder. "So why are you popping in during the middle of the day? Everything okay?"

"I am taking the rest of the week off work. To grieve."

Karen looked surprised but said nothing, patting the child.

"I... I just can't seem to pull myself together. I actually told Mayor King off today. Nicely though."

"Oh, Cass, you do need some time off. David mentioned Remi ate your shoe. How are the little guys doing?"

Cassidy laughed. "They're more in control then I am. I don't know if they're grieving Cindy or just running my life."

"Might be a little of both."

She nodded. "I have a man coming Saturday. He's very good with dogs and I think he might be able to help me sort them out. I met him at the dog park."

"So what are they doing that's so terrible? Beyond chewing your shoes?"

"I can't keep them off the bed, for starters."

Karen chuckled. "It might do you some good to have someone in your bed. Although a dog wouldn't be my first choice. Tell me about this man coming by."

"Karen! I don't need anyone in my bed, canine or human." Heat flared through Cassidy. She told herself it was indignation, but a whispering voice dared her to deny the fact sometimes her bed was lonely.

"Okay, he's cute. Handsome."

Karen switched the toddler to the other side, bouncing her knee, making the child giggle. "So which is he, cute or handsome?"

Those deep ocean blue eyes that she could leap into, that midnight hair she yearned to run her fingers through, that smile that made his eyes crinkle and the laugh that caused her tummy to flip and feel light.

"Handsome."

"Good. Glad we got that sorted out. Now, how's he going to help you with Remi and Tessa? They both went to the finest obedience school and know tons of tricks."

Cassidy sat up straight. "Really? I never knew that. Remi must have been the class drop out."

Karen scowled. "No, he did very well. They both have real diplomas too. You'd know that kind of stuff if you ever listened to Cindy when she tried to talk to you."

Remorse sliced through Cassidy. "I know. I regret it now."

"Look, honey, you'll be okay. So will they. We all just need some time." She shifted the toddler once more and reached for Cassidy's arm. "Cindy knew you loved her. I know you love me. Now let Tessa and Remi know you love them too."

Eyes misting. Cassidy nodded. She could do this.

"And while you're at it, flirt a little with this handsome man. There is no harm in that." She stopped, giving her a long study, then she smiled, snapping her fingers. "Oh yes! I know exactly what you can do. Trust me and live a little, Cassidy."

Picturing the poignant words scrawled on The Wish Wall, she mutely nodded.

~ * ~

Jake barked, tugging at the leash once he and Ethan stepped out their front door.

"What is it, buddy?" Ethan followed Jake's gaze. A moving van was parked at the apartment complex across the street. He smiled. "Ah, new neighbors coming in. Maybe they'll have a fancy poodle you can play with. Or a rough and tumble St. Bernard." He pulled the dog's leash to his side. "Or maybe they'll have two Siamese twin cats with long claws and bad attitudes. And they let them out on full moons to terrorize neighborhood pooches. Like were-cats."

He chuckled at the image. "That could make a neat cartoon. I'll keep that in reserves just in case I need it." He and Jake broke into a jog. "Just a fast run, pal, because I have to be at Miss Cassidy's by nine." He unhooked the leash and turned the dog loose once they reached the park. What were the odds she would be here as well, exercising her charges before his arrival? He unscrewed the coffee thermos and took a long swallow, wondering what she expected of him.

Ten minutes later he whistled and called for Jake. Returning home, he gave him a bone and grabbed his bike off the rack. Glancing at the moving van, he didn't see signs of movement. Well, better them than him. He'd had plenty of experience moving boxes and furniture, both for himself and friends. He'd be fine to not move anyone again for a long time.

He'd studied Cassidy's directions the night before, so he made it to her place in good time. Tying his bike to a rack in front of her apartment complex, he eased the kinks from his back and studied the front of the glass fronted, window tinted, towering building.

"Nice, Miss Cassidy. You must be making some good figures to afford this place."

A bell man greeted him as he approached the front door. "Name?" he asked after a slow appraisal up and down.

"Ethan Sheppard. To see Cassidy Grant." Which name did the guy want? His or hers? Didn't matter, he had a feeling he just failed the inspection.

Wordlessly the man turned and pressed a button on the panel behind him. "A Mr. Sheppard to see you, Miss."

"That's fine, Gisnault." Cassidy's voice came over the intercom. "Send him up please."

Still wearing a frown, Gisnault stepped aside, motioning to the stairs. "Three-twelve."

Unable to resist, Ethan gave him a snappy salute. "Got it. So, that's on the third floor?"

He felt Gisnault's frown aimed at his back until he rounded the corner. Reaching the elevator, he pressed the up button and waited. Gazing around, he spotted security cameras mounted along the hall and in the elevator vestibule. What did she do that she wanted this kind of security at home?

His place had security too. Once in a while the police cruised by while on their way to some incident. His front door opened to an outdoor walkway and the closest thing to a bellman might be the drunk who sometimes sat down at the corner. They may live only blocks away, but they were in very different neighborhoods.

Okay, no big deal. He could tell by how Cassidy dressed and her expectations of the dogs, she was out of his league. That was fine, he wasn't looking for anyone since whatshername. The fact that Miss Cassidy Grant was out of his league made it easier to keep that emotional distance. Resolved, and not knowing why, he raised his hand and pressed the doorbell.

He heard the excited barks coming from inside, then the door swung open. Vanilla, cinnamon and brown sugar reached out to pull him in. Swallowing, he followed the scents, the dogs dancing at his feet. Then he looked at Cassidy. Suddenly, he couldn't swallow. Or breathe.

"Hello."

"Hi," he said, the word sounding strangled. "Am I interrupting you?"

"Not at all. Your timing is perfect. I admire punctuality." She gestured to the table, set for two and turned back to him with a shy smile. "I thought we'd start with a good breakfast before we begin."

Begin what? Somehow, she made it sound like they were going to be doing something far different than he had originally thought. Forcing down a knot, he breathed in the heady aromas, identifying even more. Lemon. Spices. Meanwhile the dogs moved off to a lavish looking settee and lay watching them.

Apart from the intoxicating aromas of the room, Ethan swung a look around. Not that he was any expert, but he'd have to guess her taste in decorating went along with her preference in fashion, contemporary and traditional. What he could see from the flowing floor plan was clean lines, sleek furniture low to the ground, many chairs with silver metal frames. Her walls were solid, muted shades of neutral creams and soft greys. Bold pops of color burst out from the graphic prints of art she strategically placed on the walls and select pieces of decoration. Instead of looking crowded, the place appeared streamlined as an airstream trailer and orderly as a grand hotel lobby.

Except for the dogs. It was hard to miss their stuff. Ornately decorated, richly patterned and boldly colored, little doggie furniture and supplies contrasted against Cassidy's sleek, solid patterns. Aware of her waiting for him, he smothered a smile at the obvious style distinction and turned back to her. This time he was better prepared for her knock out introduction.

"So?" He swung his hands together in a clap, bringing the dog's ears up expectantly at the sharp sound.

Cassidy doled out the fluffy pancakes, a gooey icing glaze dripping off, and arranged them on two plates. She draped different fruits around the edge of another plate, carrying it and a coffee pot to the table. Done, hands curled around the chair back, she lowered her head and gave him that shy smile again.

Hot needles spiked through Ethan. He stood rooted, his body responding to Cassidy but his brain firing off red warning flares like the fourth of July. His breath came in shallow bits.

"Care to join me? Or did you want to eat all by yourself over there?"

Her soft question galvanized him, moving his feet over to the chair. He watched her pour the coffee, scents of lemons and berries rising. He lowered a fork into the thick pancake and took a bite. The abundance of warm, white cinnamon roll glaze slid down the fork to his fingers.

The flavors of sweet brown sugar, creamy powdered sugar and cream cheese, vanilla and cinnamon exploded in his mouth. They were thick enough to be cakes in their own right and light as air. Studying them, he realized they were not circular. One side held two arches and they met in a sharp point.

Were they supposed to be heart shaped? And didn't quite stay that way?

"They're so spoiled," Cassidy said, breaking into his wandering thoughts. "All their stuff, most of it over the top, and they can behave like heathens. Especially him."

By 'him', Ethan assumed she meant Remi. By herself, Tessa would probably be mellow and better behaved, but Remi lead the charge into excitement and Tessa followed.

"Well, you know us guys. We can be kind of wild. These are really good." *Except why was she making heart shaped pancakes for him?* "So was there a geometry lesson involved here somehow?" He waved his fork over the plate.

She laughed, a lilting sound that ended in a small giggle. "A failed one maybe."

The sound enthralled him, wondering what thoughts were all behind it. She'd been twirling a plump strawberry between her painted fingertips for a moment. Now, as he bit into the warm cinnamon and cream cheesy goo, she took a bite of the strawberry, their eyes catching and holding over the table.

"You don't seem so wild to me," she stated just a second before taking that bite.

His heart stopped at the sight of her lips curling over the red fruit. Why hadn't he ever noticed how lovely her lips were before? Rosy red, a slight pout even now, as she savored the flavor. In a word, they were kissable. Entirely too kissable. And now she'd taste like strawberries.

He liked strawberries.

She finished chewing, swallowing, then licked her lips. He thought he might die.

"Is everything all right, Ethan?"

He jerked to attention, sitting bolt upright in his chair. "Fine, just fine." He swallowed the bite down with the flavored coffee. Sure beat his black coffee. He might never go back to unflavored black. "So what was it you said you did? The security around here is impressive."

"I'm a city planner here in Midland." She scooped up a melon wedge.

He stiffened. "Oh? Like a court clerk kind of thing?" Needles of apprehension raced up his spine.

"No. I work with the mayor's office, doing lots of incredibly tedious and boring things. We map out long and short term goals for Midland. We work with construction, legislation, and zoning. What about you?"

Cold chills joined those needles. The food turned to paste in his mouth. "I work for *The Gazette*."

She paused. "Not as a reporter. I've never noticed you at any of the public meetings."

He shook his head. "No, we have another guy who gets to do that."

"Larger man? Both in size and personality? Wears his press badge like a police shield? Usually has a bag of chips? Always drinking some specialized coffee?"

42

"Yes, that would be him." He had to chuckle at her description of Mitch, in spite of the proximity she was swiftly gaining.

"Maybe you could help me. I have a problem I need to solve, and it's rooted within *The Gazet*te."

He went ice cold. He had to be shivering by now. "Oh?" He lifted the coffee to his lips, trying for a casual look over the rim.

"The *Punch* strip is causing me a lot of grief. Well, our leaders actually. And I need to find out who is creating it."

He froze. He very nearly spit out his coffee when she said *Punch*. Dragging in a breath, he set down his cup and reached for a strawberry, feigning nonchalance. And probably failing miserably. "Do you have terrible plans of torture in mind for this person?" He could only imagine. He took another breath, ordering himself not to shake. He reached down to grip the chair with his free hand.

"I don't know what Mr. King has in mind. It was strongly suggested I find out who that person is and pass it on." She pushed her empty plate aside. "However, I don't think it's fair to put you in that kind of conflict of interest. So if you're not comfortable sharing the identity, let's just forget it and move on."

"Okay." He gave a slow nod, willing himself to breathe again. His chest and muscles relaxed in degrees as he watched her every move under lowered lashes. He hadn't realized he'd gone so tight. What if Cassidy knew she was sitting across the table from The Salty Kidd?

She smiled, rising. "Now, these two rascals." She waved to the dogs. "Let me show you what all they have. And Remi still had to eat my shoe."

~ * ~

Cassidy wasn't sure but she'd bet she was terrible at flirting. Why had she even listened to Karen in the first place? Things were going well and suddenly Ethan looked like he was about to keel over. And it hadn't been because the cute little hearts she tried so hard to shape turned into something more like a pentagon or trapezoid. So her takeaway was to never discuss work while trying to flirt. Karen should have shared that. And how to form heart pancakes that kept their shape.

Maybe he was the janitor. That would explain his sudden discomfort.

Eager to salvage the situation, she backtracked on the flirting, and dipped back into the original business transaction. She led him around the apartment, showing him both their New Orleans Chaise red lounger and the Louis XVI Palace. How much had Cindy paid for these beds?

"And they still prefer my bed," she added.

She took him to their toy box, personalized with both a colorful "T" and "R" on both sides. "Naturally, it's overflowing with every toy ever made. And look at their closet collection. Tessa even has more nail polish than I do." Plus, she had scarves, a daisy raincoat and a pearl necklace. She hoped it was imitation pearls. "And Remi has enough coats and shirts to last a lifetime."

Ethan scrubbed his jaw, looking a little overwhelmed. "Yes, I remember seeing them wearing a lot of this stuff at the park. So what do you feed them?"

She laughed. "Organic meats, grains, vegetables and dairy. Both in their daily kibble and for the treats. Absolutely no fillers or additives. Cindy was emphatic about that. She preferred organic even in her own diet." Cindy would roll over if she knew about the vendor cart hot dogs.

"Okay, what about basic obedience? I mean, they're docile enough now."

She gave a sharp laugh. "It's because we're both here. But look what I found in their stuff." She held out two picture frames she'd unearthed from the boxes David brought over. Ethan took them, holding them at eye level, a slow grin building on his face. Heat tinged her cheeks as she wondered what he thought of them.

"They're obedience school diplomas," she finally explained.

"Yes, I see that. Top honors even. Tessa Jane Grant and Remington James Grant." He lowered them, grinning. "You weren't kidding these were her kids. Seems like your sister kept a few secrets."

No, not really, she'd just never paid any attention to know their full names or they had excelled in obedience. She shrugged. "Yeah, who knew?"

His look softened. "Given the chance, they might surprise you."

"Well, that's what you are here for. So surprise me."

Wordlessly he handed the diplomas back and regarded the dogs. He snapped his fingers. "Remi, come. Tessa, stay."

Cassidy watched. Remi dropped into a perfect sit at Ethan's feet while Tessa sat in her original place, watching eagerly.

"Remi, down." Ethan waved his hand like a magic wand.

Remi instantly dropped into a textbook down.

"Tessa, heel."

Tessa came to his left side, sitting perfectly and looking up, her short tail wagging.

"Heel." Ethan stepped across the room, both dogs pacing side by side at his heel. Mid-point he stopped and they simultaneously dropped to a sit. "Down." They plopped to their bellies, tails wagging. He returned to their original spot, both dogs glued to his side.

Next Ethan took them half way across the room, made them stay, returned to the point of origin and wordlessly called them to him with one motion of waving his arm.

Cassidy had sudden images of a snake charmer.

"Remi, bang." He held his hand out, finger pointed like a gun. Remi rolled over, covering his muzzle with his paw.

"Tessa, go back." He motioned away with a sweep of his palm.

Tessa returned to her original spot, then lay down at his downward motion. Returning to Remi, he wordlessly motioned the dog up, circle around him once and back to join Tessa in a down. Finished, he looked over at her.

Cassidy's jaw dropped.

"Who knew?" Ethan said, his amused question fanning the heat already searing her face. "So now we can conclude they do understand most of what you say."

"Yes," she agreed slowly, astounded they knew so much. "So why don't they listen?"

Ethan grinned again and took her by the elbow, cupping it gently to guide her to the sofa. Leaving a few feet between them, he shifted to face her.

"Cassidy, they are dogs, not short furry people. They will do gross

45

and seemingly crazy things that are natural for dogs. What is it exactly you expect of them?"

That stumped her. What did she expect of them? To sit there like stuffed toys and not interfere with her organized, scheduled life. How fair was that? Cindy would be crushed.

Ethan scrubbed his jaw again. "Okay, let me ask this instead, how often do you play games with them or just sit and cuddle?"

"Never," she answered softly, suspecting he spent a lot of time doing that with his bohemian dog.

"And how often do you tell them how good they are or how pleased you are with them?"

She shook her head, tears pricking her eyes. What had made Cindy think she would be the better guardian?

Ethan eased out a sigh. "Cassidy, all that they have ever known is gone. Their mama who doted on them is just gone and they don't understand why or if she's ever coming back. They are uprooted from the home they knew and I bet they don't know you very well. The routine they had known is changed. They are lost little dogs, clinging desperately to each other."

The pictures he gently painted twisted her heart. She wiped the tears away.

"Because dogs like routine, they are trying to make a new one, without much input from you. And because they are alone, feeling lost, they are going to act out, just like human children would do."

She blinked, her eyes burning as his assessment touched some nerves.

"I'm sorry because I know that's not what you wanted to hear, Cassidy, but I want you to hear the truth. Now, do you want to hear my recommendation?"

She nodded.

"Accept the fact they are here. Unless you plan on changing that, they are now a part of your life and you need to establish some house rules and clear expectations so they have someone to follow. And be forgiving when their grief or doggie habits get the better of them." He smiled. "You should also get physical with them. Get on the floor and wrestle with Remi, he'd love it. Tessa would probably just want to snuggle in your lap as you watch television. That sort of thing. Share the popcorn, invite them to become a part of your life. You might be surprised in how they change."

"I can do that, I guess." How hard could it be? Ethan made it sound so easy. She pictured him sharing popcorn with Jake. The image made her smile.

He rose to his feet and headed for the door. "Good. My work here is done. For now. Thank you for breakfast." He stopped at the door, hand on the frame, a smile on his face. "Oh yeah, one more thing, Cassidy. Let them on the bed with you once in a while. Unless there is someone else you already share it with."

Chapter Eight

"Oh, dude, I am in big trouble," Ethan bemoaned Monday morning the moment he spotted Mitch.

"You didn't call me, asking for bail, so it can't be that terrible."

He frowned. "Man, this is serious. I met that woman from the dog park on Saturday."

"And?" Mitch led the way to their office. "Did you two hit it off? Or did she hit you?"

"Both. I mean, she tried to hit on me, but she's kind of clueless how. Which was super cute and hot. It doesn't matter, anyway, because she's way out of my league. Mitch, she works for the city, under His Royal Highness I.R. King. She even knows you."

Mitch perked up, setting his coffee down. "Really? Who is she?"

Ethan explained her job and her description, then dropped into his chair. "And she wears this rolled brim red hat a lot and she smells so great and has this cute way of flicking her wrist when she talks."

"Yeah, I do know her. She's a hard tack at those meetings. The only one who yields to her is old man King himself."

Ethan didn't doubt that. In her element, she would be formidable. He gave a sad shake of his head. "She asked about the Salty Kidd, wanting to know who it was. King's hounding her to find out."

"Ouch, man, that's hitting close. What did you tell her? Did you introduce yourself and shake her hand?"

"Would you? Once she reported back to King, I'd probably be dragged through town behind his…" He paused. "What kind of car does King drive anyway?"

"A Mercedes-Benz I think. Or maybe it's a Porsche." He fished in a drawer, withdrawing a small bag of chips and ripped it open. "Something that's some crazy shade of metallic gold."

Figures. And what did Cassidy drive? If she drove. And he had a bike. Ever since he left her place Saturday he kept reliving her flirtatious attempt. While he appreciated the breakfast and the flattery, she wasn't one to flirt. She didn't have that kind of nature. And when his summary of her situation with the dogs almost made her cry, he was so tempted to pull her into his arms and kiss away those wet lashes. Except she'd probably smack him.

"At least I found out who David is. The guy's just her brother-in-law." When she mentioned that during their conversation it pleased him way more than it should have.

"Good. I was a little concerned when you started drawing his name on your storyboard. It was starting to remind me of junior high school."

~ * ~

"Okay, spill it. How'd it go?" Dana and Kelly cornered Cassidy Monday morning by the water cooler.

"Go?" Weren't they the ones who had weekend plans?

"With the dog whisperer," Kelly said, making Dana giggle.

"Oh, Ethan." Her pulse skipped a beat just saying his name. "It went well. The dogs loved him." That much was true. She slipped around them and headed for her office, aware they were both doing a great human imitation of a perfect heel. Again, she pictured Ethan leading the dogs through their skill demonstration Saturday. Her heart did a funny little flip flop.

"Come on, Cassidy, tell us all about it."

"What do you want to know? I made him breakfast and—"

"Breakfast! You made him breakfast."

"Yes, it seemed...appropriate." At the time. Thanks to Karen. Stupid heart shaped pancakes. She'd never try that again.

Dana shook her head. "This was supposed to be just a business deal. You don't normally cook breakfast for a business engagement."

"Unless you happen to run a bed and breakfast," Kelly snarked.

"Kelly, really." Cassidy spread her hands out. "I made pancakes, not a soufflé, for crying out loud. It was Karen's suggestion. And we discussed the dogs. They obeyed his every command and he gave me some pointers."

Even as Cassidy spoke, the words seemed hollow. The scenes that filled her mind all weekend were more complex than her simple explanation. Studying her friends, she knew they could tell she was holding back.

"He works at *The Gazette*," she tossed out, like when she offered Remi a bone in desperation.

Dana brightened. "Okay, now we're getting somewhere. What's he do there?"

Cassidy slumped. "I'm not sure. We never got that far."

Kelly giggled. Dana huffed a breath, crossing her arms. "Fine. What's he look like? Did you get that far?"

Heat fanning her face at Kelly's innuendo, she quickly described every feature, right down to his tight, small butt molded over faded jeans, muscular biceps rippling under his tee shirt when he hefted Remi in play, full lips as he licked the sweet cream cheese glaze off his long fingers, tender expression when he shared his opinions and those beautiful ocean blue eyes when he smiled. His voice, low and easy, flowing like a river, warmed her even now.

Kelly patted her palm over her chest, grinning at Dana. "But it was just a business engagement." They shared nods and grins, making Cassidy flush redder than her blazer.

"Ladies, if I can break in, I'd like a word with Cassidy," Adam Gaines said, his commanding voice chasing their merriment away like sunshine chased away by clouds. "Alone."

Dana and Kelly faded away, like shadows. Cassidy squared her shoulders, actually glad for the respite from her friends' questions. "Yes, Adam?"

He adjusted his tie. "I could not help but overhear your conversation. So you met with a *Gazette* employee this weekend?"

Her pulse quickened. "It was a social event, and we happened to briefly discuss our work. He offered no details, Adam. I have no clue what he does there." Though she suspected it wasn't very glamorous.

Adams waved a hand. "Doesn't matter. He's inside the enemy camp. He can give you what you need."

"Your military background is showing through, Adam. I can't force him to rat out his fellow co-workers." She stiffened, squaring her jaw. "I won't force him."

Adam Gaines pulled her next to him, his arm draped over her shoulders like a giant Anaconda. He smiled, much like a shark about to take a big bite. "Cassidy, I had a social event this weekend too, with Mayor King and his wife. And a few other political members in town. You can imagine that insane Salty Kidd and the *Punch* strip were a hot topic."

At his gentle squeeze, she nodded.

"Now, Mayor King has lit a fire under me to find out who draws that *Punch* strip. What do I have to do to light a fire under you to find out? Especially since you now have an inside man?"

~ * ~

Cassidy returned home, emotionally spent. Her feet were heavy and her steps slow as she chugged up the front walkway. She murmured a reply back to the door man, not really sure what he had said to her. With supreme effort, she reached her front door and nearly fell inside.

And directly on top of the dogs. They darted out of her way and she caught the back of the chair to stop her forward motion. Eyeing the hopeful pair, and their selected outdoor accessories, she moaned.

"Now? Can't you wait just a little while? Let me regroup first. I still have one more phone call I need to make." She dropped her purse and laptop, not caring when they thudded off the floor. Crossing to the sofa, she wearily sank down, pulling a pillow to her chest. She clutched the phone in her palm, wondering what would happen if she didn't make this call. It was to follow up with a zoning issue. The guy wanting to develop some land wasn't going to be happy with her news and right now she wasn't up to dealing with one more irritated person.

Tessa followed, slowly wagging her tail. Remembering Ethan's words, she tentatively patted to a spot beside her. "This is an invitation," she told the dog. "Take it or leave it."

Tessa bounded up, circled twice and settled down with her head on Cassidy's lap. She eased out a sigh and closed her eyes.

"I bet you used to do this with Cindy, didn't you? She probably talked to you, telling you all about her day. Well, I can tell you mine was pretty bad." She set the phone down and reached around the pillow to stroke Tessa's soft fur. "I'd have thought it would be wirier," she murmured, surprised at the soft texture. She ruffed the dog's button ears, astounded by the way they creased. Sad, but she'd never really touched them much, beyond dressing and undressing them.

"So, anyway, there is this comic strip and the mayor is getting worried about this next election. He thinks the voters will take the comic strip's messages and points against him seriously." As she recapped her predicament, her hand rhythmically swept over Tessa. "King might actually have to work to get reelected this time, thanks to all the finger pointing from *Punch*. It's making the public think and be a little more aware."

Remi trotted over, a chew rope in his mouth. Placing his front feet on the sofa, he dropped the toy next to Cassidy's free hand, pushing the phone to the edge and gave her a hopeful whine. She reached for the rope and the phone slid to the floor, bouncing on the rug. Remi snatched it up and lifted it up to her.

Accepting the phone, she set it aside, picking up his chew rope. She carefully tossed it couple of feet away and he eagerly bounded after it, only to shake it, growl once and return it to Cassidy for a replay.

"Well, it's better than my shoes or phone I suppose." She tossed it a little further and he spun around, in hot pursuit, nails clacking.

As she stroked Tessa and threw the rope for Remi and spoke about her day, Cassidy felt the tension and weight dragging at her slowly fading away. A bit of magic spun itself quietly around the room. A peacefulness filled her, chasing the dread away.

"Cindy, is this the feeling you used to talk about?" In the growing darkness, she swore she felt a gentle caress along her cheek. *Cindy?*

~ * ~

"Hold on, Buddy, we're almost there." Ethan nearly stumbled as he trotted to keep up with Jake as the dog eagerly loped down the sidewalk. Entering the gate, he barely had time to unhook the leash before Jake bounded off, barking at one of the regular dogs.

Gripping the fence for support, Ethan caught his breath and looked around for Cassidy or her dogs. Maybe they could text each other and let the other know when they were heading to the park? It was a thought. He could sell it as an excuse to check on the progress with the dogs, to see if she needed any additional tidbits of assistance.

And he could use it as a handy excuse to see her again.

"Hello, neighbor."

The familiar purring voice from behind made him spin around, the hairs on the back of his neck rising. "Neighbor?" he asked Gwen. She lived on the other end of town. Way on the other end and still too close for comfort.

She stretched like a cat, showing off her skin tight leopard print outfit. "I moved into the apartments across from you."

The moving van he'd noticed Saturday. Oh crap. He cleared his throat. He was speechless as to how to answer. No wonder she showed up with coffee.

"I could see Jake poking his head around your bedroom curtain, watching for you Saturday." She wagged a finger at him and pulled her face into a pout, unfazed by his silent horror. "Poor thing just laid there, all alone, in bed, just waiting for you."

The seductive purr in her voice made shivers crawl over him like insects. Okay, he'd have to move his bed away from the window and get inside shutters. Something that would keep her from being able to see in his bedroom. The very thought unnerved him. He liked to lie in bed and read sometimes. What if she were watching him then? A cold shudder raced up his spine.

The pout failing to work, Gwen smiled, taking a step closer, her musky, strong floral scent smothering him. "So that makes us neighbors now. Isn't that great, gorgeous?"

For once, he was scared. She'd be forever spying on him or randomly showing up at his door with coffee or whatever she dreamed up next. In the meantime, he was having nightmares just thinking about it. How hard would it be to relocate? He didn't want to move.

"I was thinking, I could make coffee and bacon for you one morning. And something else for dinner." She giggled. "And something else again for the next breakfast. Have you had pancakes lately?"

He took a step back, away from her intense floral perfume, seeking any distance. The big park suddenly seemed incredibly small. "As a matter of fact, yes, I have. I don't think you really need to be cooking anything for me, Gwen. In fact, I'd appreciate it if you just stayed away—."

"You have the prettiest blue eyes, tiger. Come to Mama." With a low growl, she thrust herself into his arms, knocking him backward and cutting off his words. Twining her hands into his hair, she dropped her lips onto his, plunging deep inside.

~ * ~

"Mitch, man, you gotta help me." Ethan caught Mitch as he shuffled up the stairs outside *The Gazette*. "I got woman trouble, big time."

Mitch chuckled. "Don't we all, buddy. So what did the power chick from the park do this time? Interrogate you with a feather tickler till you told her you were the Salty Kidd?"

Ethan winced. "Not her. Do you remember Gwen? She's like a cougar in heat. Well, she moved in across the street this weekend. She brought me coffee a few days ago and she's been watching my place. She even knows which window is my bedroom. And this morning she accosted me at the park. I swear she's following me." He needed a shower after he finally pried himself from her hooks. He almost forgot to call for Jake in his haste to escape.

"Ah, Ethan, you get all the lucky breaks. I'm jealous."

They entered their office and Ethan spun in a circle, hands balled tight. "I am not kidding. Gwen's a lion on the hunt. She's got me on her menu. She even makes me feel like a hunk of beef. I barely escaped her clutches today."

Mitch studied him, a grin on his face. "So I'm still not seeing the being in trouble part."

Ethan slugged his arm. "I'm thinking I might have to move out of my place. I like my place."

"Yeah, I'm not itching to help you move again either." Mitch tilted his head to one side. "Or you could just stop going to the park. That way the lioness couldn't touch you. Unless you open your door."

That might work, except he needed to be able to step out his door. And if he stopped going to the park, how would he ever see Cassidy again? This stalking thing was way out of hand. Not only was it affecting his nerves, making him feel he had to constantly look over his shoulder for Gwen, it was compromising how he might be able to see Cassidy.

He shook his head. "I like the park. Jake likes the park. His buddies are all there."

Mitch pulled out another bag of chips and tore it open. "True enough. So what are you going to do?"

"I don't know. That's what I need your help for." Ethan dropped into his chair, burying his head in his hands, listening to the loud sounds of Mitch's crunching.

"Well, I suppose you could get a warrant of some kind against her. One of those anti-stalking things."

Well, there was a good suggestion. Why hadn't he thought of that? Ethan cracked a smile. "I knew you were useful for something besides eating chips and feeding me town gossip." He'd probably have to go down to the police station, which was next door to city hall and the mayor's offices. Cassidy's domain. What were the chances of bumping into her?

"I'll go just before lunch. Thanks. I owe you."

Chapter Nine

Cassidy cradled the laptop as she and the lawyer and his assistant studied the screen. The assistant, a leggy blond with a mile high hairdo, dragged her painted fingernail along the screen and highlighted sections to the old lawyer at her side. Finally, he made some comments and Cassidy closed the laptop.

"Thank you for meeting me on such short notice," she said, nodding to both the lawyer and his assistant. "Adam has been anxious to get further confirmation on this so we can move forward. He will be glad for your insight."

Armed with new knowledge for the latest proposal Adam handed her, she headed back down the hall. It was nice outside, so she'd take the scenic route back to the offices next door. It was pure luck, and a chance tip, that she caught the lawyer while he was filing some paperwork at the jail. Once she handed this information over to Adam, she could take it off her plate. If only every task were this easy to cross off. She still had no clue how she was going to figure out who that Salty Kidd was.

She refused to involve Ethan any further than what had already been discussed. Perhaps she could go to the *Gazette* office in person and discuss the matter with the publisher.

"Cassidy?"

Spinning, she drew in a breath. "Ethan? What are you doing here?" While he looked just like he always did, comfortably casual and sinfully sexy, how did she look? She was wearing a new blouse Cindy had bought for her birthday this year and never worn, thinking it too delicate for work. After last night, she decided to take the chance. Warming under his intense gaze, she was glad she pulled it from the closet this morning. She paired it with mid-calf heeled boots and a pleated skirt reaching to her knees. To judge by Ethan's initial expression, it must look okay.

He rammed his hands in the pockets of his faded jeans and gave her both a shrug and grin. "I came here to file some paperwork. How about you?"

What kind of paperwork would he be filing at a jail? "I work next door. One of the lawyers working on a current legislation proposal was here and I needed a quick consult."

She shifted, her heels clinking on the hard tile floor as she stared into his eyes. "Is everything alright?"

"I hope so." He paused. "Look, it's lunch time and I'm starved. How about I treat you to something? *Mustard's Last Stand* isn't far."

She smiled. The hot dog place was popular among her co-workers but she'd never been that thrilled with it. Lunch with Ethan did sound tempting. Surely Adam could wait a little while to get this information?

"All right, but how about somewhere else? Have you been to *Basic Kneads Breads?* They do a fantastic grilled cheese."

The hopeful smile on his face spread till his eyes crinkled and he reached for her elbow. "No, can't say I've been there, but I sure am game to try. Who doesn't love a good grilled cheese? Which direction?"

She could not help smiling to herself as she and Ethan walked side by side in the warm sunshine. Flowers filled the air with their fragrance. A few pigeons wobbled around, pecking for crumbs along the sidewalk. Suddenly the two blocks to the diner seemed incredibly short.

Moments later Ethan guided them to a small table in the crowded diner. Cassidy set her laptop bag next to her and rested her hands on the table. Ethan propped one elbow on the tabletop, whipping up a menu with the other.

"Yes, lots of variations on the standard old grilled cheese. The brisket with mac and cheese with cheddar on sourdough sounds pretty good."

That didn't surprise her. He'd go for a mile high sandwich. "I like the apple and arugula with poached salmon and goat cheese on ciabatta bread." It was one of her favorites.

They placed their orders, opting to share a basket of sweet potato fries and sliced sweet apples.

"So how are things going with the pooches?"

"Good. Better." She recounted the sofa episode. "I swear Cindy was there."

"I wouldn't be surprised if she was. She loved the dogs and she loved you." He leaned forward, brushing away a wisp of hair that escaped her bun. "I bet it gets hard sometimes."

"Mostly the guilt." She gave a sad laugh. "Karen says I'm too hard on myself, but I know the truth."

Ethan shrugged, his eyes soft, like waves lapping onto the shore under the moonlight. A shiver moved up Cassidy's spine.

"You seem kind of unsettled," Ethan finally observed. "Is there anything else bothering you?"

She drew in her lower lip. Did she dare? It had been bad the last time she mentioned it. She swore she wasn't going to mention it again. It wasn't fair to him. She glanced around the room, not seeing any city hall workers. Given his behavior last time, and despite his position at the paper, he had to know something. Anything. Even if he just emptied the person's trash, it was a bone she could throw at Adam. It wasn't that large of a paper.

"There is, but I don't think you want to hear about it."

"Try me," he immediately challenged, leaning forward.

She could not resist his direct dare. "It's about *Punch*. My boss is really putting the pressure on me to find out who draws it. The mayor is pretty worked up, especially after the love lock issue came up. Other things too, but that's kind of when it started to be a serious thorn in his side. And now it seems lodged in mine."

She paused, as their plates were set before them, steam rising and smells of browned bread and melting cheese filling the space around them. "I meant what I said before, about not wanting to put you in an awkward spot. I respect your loyalty to *The Gazette*." She paused again, drawing another breath. "But if you'd like to share a name or two, I would really appreciate it. To be honest, it might mean my job."

Ethan leaned back, a mixture of deep emotions in his eyes. He rested both hands on either side of his plate, a haggard weariness building on his face. "Let me think about it, okay?"

~ * ~

"He's not going to do it," Cassidy declared.

Karen dabbed the spit up cloth around the face of baby in the stroller, eased back with a sigh and studied her sister. "You don't know that."

"I do know that. He isn't going to do it."

"Have you suddenly turned clairvoyant? If so, please tell me the winning lottery numbers."

Cassidy spared her sister a frown before turning her attention back to the racing kids and dogs. They met at the park, to enjoy a sunny afternoon and let everyone have a good run. Karen had called and mentioned the kids were restless so Cassidy suggested this.

"If he's as into you as you think, he will share what he knows. But it might not be the name of who it is. Maybe he just knows where their office is or something."

"He may be into me, but he's also into his job. Whatever it is."

"The Salty Kidd," Karen mused, handing a bright toy to the toddler beside them. "What kind of pseudonym is that anyway?"

"The pseudonym of someone who is going to get me fired."

Karen huffed a breath. "You're not going to get fired, because he is going to tell you what he knows. And besides, they can't fire you over something as silly as this. You could sue them."

"Sue the town of Midland?"

"Sure. People probably do it all the time."

The melody of an ice cream truck reached them. Within moments the colorful van, white with giant blue, yellow, pink and green dots, rolled up nearby. Karen and Cassidy watched as two greatly overweight women waddled up to the van, waving bills. Within a moment they both toddled away, towering triple cones in hand. The sisters shared amazed grins.

"Stay here and watch the dogs. I'll buy ice cream for everyone." Standing up, Cassidy called for her older niece and nephew to join her. "Pick your flavors, guys. And I'll also take a chocolate cone and a tutti-fruity please." She handed over her money as the kids clamored for their favorite flavors. Soon they raced away, licking their cones. Cassidy returned to Karen and handed over the chocolate ice cream.

"Thanks. You just made those kids happy." She offered a sample to the cooing toddler.

"Don't thank me too fast. I stole a lick of yours."

~ * ~

Cassidy and Dana arrived at Eddie's party. Even though they were ahead of time, the house was already overflowing with people. Streamers fluttered in the breeze, marking the entry way. Strands of music filtered out the open windows.

"Pop music, my favorite kind," Dana said, tugging at Cassidy's hand. "There's Kelly."

"Wow, some crowd," Cassidy pointed out once they caught up with Kelly.

Kelly smiled, her body already moving to the beat of the music. "Yeah, I don't even know half the people here. Come on in."

Entering, Dana broke off, heading for the appetizer table as she muttered something about being starved. Cassidy glanced around, waving to a few friendly faces she recognized from work. Most of the guests she did not know. Kelly once more grabbed her arm and pulled her to the makeshift dance floor where the furniture had been pushed away.

"It's upbeat, Cassidy, you don't have to dance with any one person."

Loosening up, she twisted and wiggled like Kelly, giggling along with a group of other men and women. Space was tight, making it impossible to stay with one partner. Indeed, she spent more time facing Kelly than the other dancers.

Eddie rounded a corner, a beaming smile on his face. He spread his hands out toward the group. Suddenly the music dimmed.

"Welcome one and all. I am so delighted to see everyone. Thank you for coming to my event. I'd like to give a shout out to my friends who helped me organize and set this up. Let's hear it for Chris and Tony."

Cassidy swiveled around, trying to spot the two friends. Not recognizing them either, she clapped along with the rest and returned her attention back to the rotund speaker, Eddie.

"So we have snacks and drinks over there." He waved to the two tables Dana had bee-lined too. "We have dancing in here, obviously. And through that doorway we have an area set up for some really cool games. If you want to know which ones, you'll have to come follow me." He cued the music. "Again, I am so glad you all could make it. Relax and enjoy." Turning, he started back from where he had come, beckoning others to follow him.

"Come on, Cassidy," Dana urged, shoving a cheese loaded cracker in her mouth before grabbing Cassidy's arm.

She looked to Kelly, who was weaving to the beat.

"Nope, I'm staying in here," Kelly announced. "Dancing's totally my thing."

Catching the excitement of the room, and Dana's hopeful smile, she relented. "Okay, to the games we go."

Chapter Ten

They filed in with about half a dozen other people. Eddie was waiting, still beaming and waved them to chairs scattered in groups.

"Come in, find a spot. Get comfy. We've got some great games planned."

"Hi there. Care if I join you ladies?"

Cassidy turned, slowly looking up, her breath hitching. *Ethan.* "What are you doing here?" she asked.

He shrugged. "Friend of a friend of one of the friends." He slid down next to Cassidy and extended his hand to Dana. "Hi, I'm Ethan Sheppard."

"Dana Slawicki. Pleased to meet you." Dana pumped his arm. "Cassidy has been very closed mouthed about you."

Ethan grinned, cutting a bemused smile at Cassidy, who grew warm from her hair roots to her toes. "Really?" Ethan asked, lifting a dark brow in question.

"Yes, all she said is you two met at a dog park."

"We did," he confirmed. Cassidy tuned her attention to Eddie as he explained the first game, trying to ignore the whispered conversation between Dana and Ethan. Fortunately, Eddie's booming voice drowned them out as he held up a jar and a stack of slips of paper.

"It's called *Questions.* Everyone writes one question down and drops it in this old mayonnaise jar. Then we pass the jar back around and each person draws out one slip of paper and has to answer the question. Others can help offer answers too, that's half the fun. The other half is you have to be truthful about answering the question you draw." He laughed and handed the materials to the person nearest to him.

Dana and Ethan continued their conversation, with Dana driving it with questions of her own, while they waited for the jar and paper. The guest across from Cassidy handed the items over and she balanced them all on her lap. Thoughtfully nibbling her lip, she wrote a question down, folded it carefully and dropped it in the jar. Giving it a shake, she handed it to Dana. She watched as Dana and Ethan took their turns writing down their questions and passing the jar on.

Finally, it came back to Eddie, who dropped his own question in and shook the jar vigorously. He then handed it back to the person closest to him.

"Okay, if you could travel through time, to anywhere, where would it be and why?"

Answers came forth, mostly for votes of going forward in time for the advancements of medicine and technology. Cassidy peeked over at Ethan, to see him studying her with a contemplative stare.

"Right here is pretty good," he said, a smile stretched over his lips.

Beside her, Dana giggled. She jabbed her elbow into Dana's side.

"I'd like to go back to the roaring 20's," the guest who drew the question said and handed the jar on. "It was a prosperous and fun-loving time. Styles were important."

"Okay, next question. If you could sneak anything into your rental lease, what would it be?"

Once more, answers came out from the crowd. "New appliances."

"Free rent on your anniversary month."

"Birthday cake."

Again, Cassidy glanced over at Ethan, warming at his soft smile trained on her. He wasn't really getting into the game, but he seemed to be enjoying her presence. A pleasant sensation poured down over her.

"I'd like to have written permission to have a pet because my current lease doesn't allow them," the drawer supplied, handing the jar over.

"If you could be any animal, what would it be?

"A cat, because they are slinky and sleek."

"A dog because they are loyal and smart."

"A horse, so I could race up and down the streets and the police couldn't do anything about it."

Obviously that person liked to speed and probably had the ticket collection to prove it.

"If you were mayor for the day, what three things would you change about the city?" was the next question drawn out.

Cassidy's breath hitched. Who could have thought of that question? She glanced at Dana, who shrugged, her lips turned up into a sly smirk. *Dana!*

She glanced around, carefully looking at the guest's expressions as they considered their answers.

"Collect as much taxes as possible."

"Have a big parade, in my honor."

"Decorate the whole city in bright lights and colorful streamers."

"Forgive everyone's speeding tickets."

Clearly Speedy has some issues.

"Make all the restaurants give free food to the homeless," the drawer supplied. "And have a day each month where people could get free health screenings at the hospital." She shrugged, handing the jar on. "That's all I can think of."

Cassidy turned to Ethan, who had so far been quiet. "What would you do?" she asked softly, keenly aware of Dana's open curiosity

He leaned close, near enough for her to inhale his spicy scent. "You don't want to know."

A chill raced up her spine, both at his solemn answer and the smoky look in his dark eyes.

"Oh, this is a good question," another guest said, after unfolding his note. "If you could change someone's life for the better, at a cost of ruining your own, would you do it?"

No instant answers shouted out this time. Guests glanced at one another, thoughtful expressions on their faces. Cassidy looked at Ethan and instantly cooled at his attentive expression. Was this his question?

"Would you?" he asked softly, looking deep into her eyes, touching her heart.

"I—I don't know." Others murmured their answers but she never heard them. Her pulse skipped a few beats and her lips parted. What was he implying? Lost in the depths of his eyes, she tried to find her voice. "W…would you?"

"If I were man enough."

Dana got the jar next. "Umm, how many kids do you want?" she read, lips twitching, eyes on Cassidy. "I want five," she declared, as if daring Cassidy.

Various numbers came forth from others. Cassidy felt herself get lost in Ethan's eyes. "How many?" she whispered, her heart thumping wildly.

He gave a shrug, also armed with a sly smile. "Two or three sound good."

Dana handed the jar to her. Willing her fingers not to shake, she pulled out a paper. Reading it, her breath expelled in a rush. Unable to meet his stare, she sought out Dana instead.

"Do you believe in love at first sight?"

Grinning widely, Dana nodded. "Yes."

"Yes," Ethan rumbled. Hearing the humor in his tone, she closed her eyes, heart beating like the wings of a caged bird.

"You have to tell the truth," Eddie reminded her.

Damn. "Yes," she bit out, thrusting the jar to Ethan.

He withdrew a paper, his smile growing as he read it. "How would you describe your dream date?"

Though he read it to the group, it was aimed at Cassidy. Somehow the game had become just between them. Her breathing stopped. Her pulse raced. Her skin tingled. Answers came around the room, but as though from a distance. She licked her lips, knowing he waited for her. Beside her, Dana sat in rapt attention.

"It would be perfect," she finally decided. "Perfect location, perfect food, perfect ambience and the perfect events."

He smiled, his eyes hooded. "With the perfect partner."

Another chill slithered up Cassidy's spine. The room suddenly felt warm. "With no secrets between them."

He slowly nodded. "With no secrets between them. And eventually, no clothes either."

Who knew cold chills of excitement would make a body heat up so hot?

"I… I need to go outside a moment." Lurching to her feet, she shot for the door. Bolting past the dancers weaving around the impromptu dance floor, she pushed the front door open. Gulping in breaths of fresh air, she leaned against a post on Steve's porch, eying the moonlight and stars beyond.

"Are you all right?" Ethan's warm hand landed on her shoulder and she flinched. "Fine. I just needed some air." *And to get away from the heated desire in your eyes.*

Turning slowly, she steeled herself for that desire again. This time concern filled his eyes as he rested his hands lightly on her shoulders.

"If I made you uncomfortable, with anything I said or did, I'm sorry."

Her heart splintered and she shook her head. "You didn't." How could he be responsible for her body's reactions?

Music drifted out, surrounding them. Stars shone brightly, sparkling in his eyes. New emotions rained down around Cassidy, reminding her she'd been alone—and lonely—for too long.

"Feeling better?"

She wet her lips and nodded. "Would you rather stay out here or go back inside? We could take a walk. Or join the next game they're playing."

He smiled, his teeth white in the moonlight. "I'd rather stay here and dirty dance alone with you."

His words, coupled with his gentle touch, slammed into her. Waves of heated desire and even hotter need throbbed through her like the beating drums filtering through the window screens.

"I want to kiss every inch of your skin."

His rumbling purr chased away any last inhibition. She kicked off her shoes, pushing them aside. Taking his hands into hers, she looked deep into his eyes, dark with a desire matching her own. Heart beating a rapid tattoo, she smiled up at him. Catching the rhythm of his racing heart, she swayed.

Soon he took the lead, lowering his head to nuzzle along her exposed neck. Shivers of excitement pulsed over her. She held her breath as he rained kisses along her neck, collarbone and under her blouse to her shoulder. Plying her blouse aside, he dragged his tongue back along, to tickle at the base of her throat, and slowly, achingly, move up by gradual inches to claim her lips.

Fire licked over Cassidy. She fought to draw a breath. Had his hands not been caressing her, she'd surely fall. She'd danced with men before, but none had ever had this effect on her like Ethan did.

Finally, the song inside ended and they stopped, their bodies still scant inches apart. Ethan studied her, a crooked smile on his lips. "Well, it seems we have the perfect location, ambience and partner. And all the other perfect requirements we need. That just leaves us the clothing issue to have our dream date."

She swallowed. What if they danced like that again, only naked? To feel his hard, toned and hot body sliding against her? If the lava engulfing her now was any indicator, she knew where it would certainly lead. It was the stuff of her dreams. She nodded. "Yes, it does. And the secrets."

His eyes darkened to black as the evening sky. "Yes…and the secrets."

Chapter Eleven

Ethan leaned back in his chair, his feet propped on the desk and the window open to the breeze and smells of car exhaust. He tossed the quarter up, watched it spin and glitter in the sunlight and then caught it deftly on his wrist as it fell. Covering it, he paused before lifting to peek. Sighing, he gave it another flip, to set it sailing upward to repeat the process. Again.

"Heads."

Mitch's arrival startled him, breaking into his reverie. The coin fell, clinking on the floor. "What?" he asked, bending to retrieve it, the chair squeaking.

"I'm calling heads." Mitch nodded to the coin. His own chair groaned as he settled into it. "So what are we betting on anyway? Next ball game?"

"What method I die by."

"You know, there is a built in glitch about proving you're the winner on something like that," Mitch said, tilting his head to consider the bet. "How about sexual exhaustion? It's every man's fantasy."

"Yours maybe." Ethan dropped the quarter back in the pencil drawer and picked out a pencil. Hovering it over his board, he stilled. Next to him came the familiar scent of cheese and well-known crunching and rattling sounds.

"I'm thinking of telling Cassidy I'm the Salty Kidd."

Mitch paused. "Yup, that might certainly lead to your premature death. Why?"

"Why not? She's asking me for a name."

"So make something up. You're creative. Give her another false name, but one that sounds generic and makes some sense this time. Like, uh, Joe Smith. Or Tom Jones. Lots of them around."

"That would be lying. Which would be worse than not saying anything." He exchanged the pencil for another. "I met her at that party last night, the one you told me about. Doug's friend, Chris. You should have gone. Cassidy and her girlfriends were there and a bunch of us played this game, called *Questions*." He blew out a breath. "Man, she was sexy as could be, especially when we got some of those questions."

Mitch perked up. "Yeah? Like what?"

"Like how many kids we wanted. Visions of our perfect date. Someone even asked what we would do if we were mayor for the day. I think that one was from her co-worker, mixing a little business in with the fun." He grinned. "For supposedly being a fun game, there sure were some hard questions."

"So how many kids do you want?"

He shot Mitch a look. "Two point three. And a house in the suburbs. What does it matter?"

"Umm, don't forget about the dog. To go with those two point three kids."

"I think we've got that covered already." Murmuring, he turned back to the blank storyboard. He was supposed to be creating. Why was it suddenly so difficult? Why was his creative mind abruptly so…bare?

"You know, I think it's a rebound thing." Mitch declared.

Ethan spared him one darting glance. "What is?" He still had not made a mark on the page. How could his storyboard be so blank when his thoughts were so full? This was going to kill him.

"This woman who has you so discombobulated."

He smiled. "Is that what you see me as?" He wasn't aware that was even a word in Mitch's vocabulary. He'd bet he couldn't spell it.

"Yeah. I think you're still bummed out about whatshername stranding you at the altar, so you're vulnerable now. Sure you handled it well, but subconsciously it's simmering and festering. Little Miss At-the-Park and her cute pint-size puppies are grabbing your heart now because it's up for grabs."

Ethan set his pencil down and swiveled to face Mitch. "That's an interesting theory, pal, but I can dispute it so easily." He snapped his fingers. "If I were rebounding, or vulnerable, Gwen would have snatched my heart up long ago. Cassidy isn't even trying, whereas that crazy Gwen is trying every trick in the book, plus a few she wrote as well. How do you explain that?"

Mitch shrugged and bit into another chip. "So how'd it go down at the police station anyway?"

He sighed. "Apparently not too many men sign out stalking warrants against women. I got a few strange looks and had to explain myself a couple times. One guy even thought I was turning myself in for a stalking warrant against me. You have no idea how close I came to being arrested." He shook his head. "I ran into Cassidy afterwards. We went out to lunch." He took a deep breath. "You should have seen the outfit she was wearing. All polished professional and sexy as hell. She had just enough lace and curls to look ultra-feminine but still keep that official at-the-office look."

"Yeah, she's a sharp dresser. Like she's saying: Look at me, but don't even think of touching all this." He ran a hand up and down himself, like a model featuring a new design.

Ethan nodded, smiling at the memory of her outfit, reliving the heart-racing emotions and breath-stealing thoughts from the party, before he uttered a sigh and shot Mitch a somber look. "And her boss is burning hot to find out who the Salty Kidd really is. She says it might mean her job."

"Yeah, but, Ethan, telling her might mean your job too."

~ * ~

Cassidy sank deep into the sofa, a long sigh escaping her like steam from a radiator. It seemed every bone in her body ached. And her head throbbed. And her pulse still raced. Now she knew how a hunted deer felt.

"You want to know why?" she asked the dogs standing at her feet. "Because Mayor King suddenly has me in his sights." Her dad used to go deer hunting, so she remembered hearing him use the language of the hunter. It had been his escape from a houseful of females. "And instead of protecting me, like a good boss should, Adam is placing a bullseye target on my back." Fishing her phone from her pocket, she eyed it once and set it further out of reach. Safe from Remi's reaching paws.

She dragged a soft throw from the back of the sofa and draped it over her legs. That was a cue to Tessa who leapt up, circled twice and lay down, head resting on Cassidy's knee. Remi raced to his toy box and returned with a braided rope, dropping it on the edge of the blanket.

"Okay, I'm getting the picture, you two." Stroking Tessa with one hand, she tossed the rope with the other. Remi spun and took off in pursuit, growling and giving it a few savage shakes once he grabbed it.

"I'd hate to think what you would do if you ever caught something alive. Cindy said your breed was supposed to hunt little furry things." Or snakes. Or anything else they happened upon. It had been one of the conversations they had before Cindy got sick. Back when she was so excited to share her knowledge of her new baby to her sisters.

Closing her eyes, she tossed the rope again and drifted back to that day. She and Karen had joined at Cindy's house, sharing tea and sandwiches, and exclaiming over how cute Remi the puppy was. Even then, while she enjoyed the visit with her sisters, she was glad to leave and return to work. She had some paperwork to complete before a big meeting the next morning.

"Back then, I had no idea how fleeting those visits were going to be," she murmured to Tessa. "And I certainly had no idea one day you two would be living in my house. I swear, I never expected Cindy to leave." She tossed the rope again, Remi's nails clacking as he raced over the floor. "I bet you didn't either."

She clicked on the television, not caring what show it landed on. Laughter spilled out into the room. She didn't bother looking at the screen. Her hand rhythmically caressed Tessa's ears. "When you met me, did you have any idea one day your mommy would die and leave you to my care? Me, of all people, expected to care for two dogs. Cindy sure had a sense of humor."

Tessa tensed, ears perking up as she stared intently at a spot in the room.

"What's the matter? Do you hear something?" Even Remi stopped chewing his toy and gazed at the same spot. A chill crept over Cassidy. There was nothing there, nothing different. Still, she turned down the television. At a low whine from Remi, and a wag of his tail, she turned it off. Tessa crept closer to Cassidy, whining softly.

Cassidy rested her hand on Tessa. "Are you guys missing your mom? What do you think about at times like this? It's been a month now." It was hard to believe a whole month had passed. Sometimes she still felt like she was in a bad dream. She turned her gaze to where they both stared. A sob built up inside her, burning her chest.

"Can you believe it's been a month since your lives changed forever? I bet you never dreamed you'd be here with me." She swallowed the sobs.

"I bet you never thought your mommy would go away like she did." A tear, hot and salty, slid down her face. "Me neither."

A softness touched her cheek, blowing past like a feather on a breeze. She reached up, pressing her fingertips to her cheek and closed her eyes. Tears ran unchecked, leaving wet trails.

"Cindy, I'm trying, really I am. I miss you so much and wish I'd taken the time I should have when you were here. Forgive me?"

She felt a kiss press to her nose and a hand brush through her hair. Tessa gently climbed fully onto her lap and licked her tears. Cassidy pulled Tessa to her chest, hugging her warm furry body tightly. Remi leaped up to snuggle next to them.

~ * ~

"Cassidy? Join us for lunch?" Kelly popped her head in. Cassidy looked up from the computer. Dana waved at her from behind Kelly. Was it that time already? Where had her morning gone?

"Sure. Where to?" She saved her email, locked the screen and grabbed her purse.

"How about *Basic Kneads*? Dana's never been."

Something, and she wasn't sure what it was, knifed through Cassidy. She still carried those memories of her and Ethan's lunch fresh in her mind.

"Or we could go somewhere else?" Dana suggested slowly.

"No, that's fine." She must really be transparent. After last night, she was probably an open book to everyone. She finally cried herself to sleep on the sofa, and awoke later to find Tessa still nestled contentedly in her arms and Remi curled over her feet.

It took some effort but she disengaged them enough to slip out from under them. Restless, she took them for a fast walk to the park, under the streetlights. Returning home, she gave them extra treats and finally crawled into bed. Within seconds, they joined her. This time she didn't even try to get them to move.

She could never try to explain what happened last night to others. They'd think she was crazy. Ethan had understood, gently accepting it for what she thought it was. Cindy.

"*Basic Kneads* is good," she assured her friends. They walked along the sunshine filled sidewalk, mingling with bikers and strollers, with Kelly and Dana talking non-stop about the party.

"I thought you two were going to go for it right there," Dana said. "On Steve's floor."

She shook her head, growing warm under the bright sunlight. It suddenly felt like an interrogation light. "We're not like that," she defended herself. "He just helps me with the dogs."

Dana and Kelly shared grinning looks. "Uh huh. And that's our Cassidy, still living in Denial Land. That guy wants you as bad as you want him. And he's a sexy hot hunk."

She picked up the pace. "Yes, he's hunky, but I doubt he wants me. It's not like that."

"Right, girlfriend."

They finally arrived and Kelly guided them to a table three away from the one Cassidy and Ethan had shared. She gave it a glance, sweeping over the young couple currently seated, giggling over a basket of hot cross buns.

"Do you know them?" Dana asked.

"What? Oh, no. I just…thought they looked familiar. But they don't." She yanked her concentration back to her friends.

"Did your time off help much, Cassidy?"

"Maybe. It's hard to put a timeline on something like this." She took a drink of her water. "Karen and I are both moving along at our own pace. She has David and the kids to occupy her mind. I have… Cindy's dogs." And apparently spectral visits and that overwhelming guilt that Karen didn't have.

"When our parents died, it was different. They were already divorced, Karen and I were in college. Cindy was a teen, living with Mom." She rested her hands on the table, noticing how Dana and Kelly were leaning into her memories. "We lost Dad first. He had an accident where he worked. Mom got the call, and she contacted Karen and me. Mom developed cancer years later. Cindy was in college by then. Karen was newly married and I was already working here. She was determined to fight it, had all the normal stuff done and ultimately, still died, a couple years later."

It had seemed surreal then. The cancer was just a start, leading to further complications and problems that eventually led to her death. The only consolation was they all had time to prepare themselves mentally. Time to say good bye.

"With Cindy, it was different. She was the baby. She was diagnosed and gone within just a few months. She said she'd fight it just like Mom had, and we figured there would be time to find a cure or whatever." No one, at least her, expected it to happen so quickly. If so, she would have…been there. Right?

Kelly reached over and patted her arm. "Don't stress it, Cassidy. You'll stop hurting one day. So how are things really going with that hunky dog whisperer?"

Chapter Twelve

"Hi, I'm taking Jake to the park now. Have you taken Tessa and Remi yet?"

Cassidy's heart skipped a few beats at Ethan's soft voice. Then her pulse raced at the possible reasons of why he was calling to ask such a question. Her grip tightened on the phone. "Not yet. Remi seems to be, well, slow. For him anyway."

"Is he okay?"

Her dog whisperer. "I guess so. I think he ate something that didn't agree with him." Probably someone's ice cream. "Frankly, it's a bit of a relief." She chuckled.

"Well, I would be glad to take a look at him. I'm no vet, of course, but I can usually tell if it's serious enough to see a vet or if it's something that can be cared for at home."

"Like two aspirin and an ice pack to the head?"

He laughed. "Yeah, something like that."

"Okay, we can meet you at the park. How does twenty minutes sound?"

"Perfect."

With a new found burst of energy, Cassidy finished dressing Tessa and opted to skip Remi's outerwear. Last night she had painted Tessa's nails, and hers, a coordinating shade of pearl pink. She slipped on Tessa's pearl collar. "Now, don't you look pretty?"

Standing up, she glanced in the mirror. There was no doubt Ethan liked her dogs, but how much of his interest was in just her?

Reaching the park, she unhooked them and watched as Remi made a pitiful attempt at a full-throttle dash.

"His usual zest doesn't seem to be there, does it?"

Whirling, she stared into Ethan's eyes, pulse galloping at her own accelerated speed. Jake danced around them once and bolted, quickly meeting his larger pals at the far end of the fence.

Ethan reached for her arm and she followed him to a nearby bench. Sitting down, they silently watched the dogs race around. Nearby a grandfather wearing suspenders was playing Red Light, Green Light with two little boys. They watched them a moment, smiling at the hearty laughter of the Grandpa and giggles of the children.

"You look nice today. About Remi, has he vomited anything?"

A compliment and bodily functions. Cassidy wasn't sure she liked them sandwiched together in the same conversation. Yet Karen often did that with the kids. Maybe it was just a parent thing.

"Thank you, and no he hasn't. I met Karen here for ice cream the day before yesterday and I think he stole some from the kids. And he got into my leftover lunch last night. Some friends and I went to *Basic Kneads* and I brought part of a taco sandwich home." For a dog with his level of obedience training, it was nothing short of dumbfounding to her that he was such a mischief maker.

He grinned. "Yep, that could certainly do it, more so than a few stolen licks of the ice cream."

She hesitated, lowering her gaze. "And last night I painted Tessa's nails. Later on, I noticed him nibbling on her feet."

He shot her a startled glance and she quickly curled her own pink nails into her palms. Looking around, he blasted a whistle across the park and called for Tessa. In mid-roll, she scrambled up and raced to him. He praised her, hoisted her up and checked her feet, chuckling softly.

"Very nice. This shade matches her collar too. Apparently, Remi decided they were also edible. Look."

Sure enough. Her hard work to layer the strokes so even had been a wasted effort. Tessa's pink nails were reduced to scratches and zig zag lines. "She looks like a punk rocker," she said in dismay. "All she needs now are neon stripes in her fur."

"It's been done to dogs, believe it or not." He released Tessa with a friendly pat and leaned back as she trotted off. He spread an arm out, just missing her shoulder. She had the insane urge to inch closer, so that they could touch.

"I think he'll be okay once his tummy settles down. Maybe keep them apart till her nails are dry the next time you two do the pedicure thing." He cut her a mischievous grin. "That shade looks good on you too."

Heat shot through her and she unfurled her hands, exposing the nails in silent confession. Whatever he did at *The Gazette*, he was observant. Enough so, he probably knew the identity of the Salty Kidd. Did she dare ask whether he'd considered her request?

"Any special plans for today?"

Her thoughts instantly shifted. "Yes, Mayor King has a special project coming up. He is surveying neighborhoods who have Love Locks and other forms of public expression to see the various opinions of the residents. My boss wants me to go around town and note what neighborhoods have these expressions and which ones. That way we can better target our surveys."

"Is this all for the upcoming election?"

"Indirectly. The information gained will better tell the Mayor how his constituents feel about certain issues."

"So he knows how to respond as election time draws near."

She studied his tight profile. "I take it you are not a fan of Mayor King."

He laughed, short and dry. "I don't think he's a fan of me."

"What do you mean by that?" He personally knew King? She'd never seen him at any of their social functions or public events. He surely didn't sound like a casual friend of the family and his age wasn't right to have dated any of King's female relatives.

"So how are you going to do this city-wide neighborhood tour? Certainly, not by bus?"

She expelled a breath. Clearly, he wasn't going to answer her. "No. I think I'll drive around, park, walk a bit, make some notes and drive some more. That ought to take me most of the day." And one very long, lonely day.

He brightened, his tension melting. "All by yourself? That could have some inherent drawbacks. Isn't anyone able to go with you?"

"No, there isn't anyone available." She'd asked for either Kelly or Dana but Adam refused to let them out of their obligations for the day. "Why?"

He fiddled with the leash at his belt loop. "I could go with you. For safety sake. And companionship. I could help with the note taking and even buy you lunch. It seems much safer, and more pleasant, than you just trekking alone all over town."

His offer did sound good. Images of traveling the town, and lunch, with him flitted through her mind, hot on the reminders of their dancing at the party. Adam wouldn't care, would he? He'd never even need to know. She'd still get the assignment done.

"Your boss doesn't mind you just taking off like this? Don't you have a job to go to today?" Even if it was just emptying out the trash.

He shrugged. "As long as I can get the work done on time, my boss is pretty lenient on the details." He gave her a hopeful smile. "What do you say, Cassidy?"

Again, she wondered at his occupation but was more interested in his soft, winsome expression. Her pulse sky-rocketing again, she felt herself nodding in agreement. "How about I come pick you up at your place in half an hour?"

He hesitated a full breath, then relaxed and nodded. "Okay." He gave her brief directions and stood, helping her to her feet, hands lingering as he searched her face. Before she could question him, he pulled her into his arms and gently tipped her chin upward. Touching his lips to hers, he caught one hand in his and curled the other arm around her shoulder, searing her back with his heated touch.

She melted, molding herself under his touch. Her lips tasted the coffee he'd recently drank. His skin smelled like aftershave. His dark hair was thick beneath her roving fingers. Her heart broke into a wild gallop as he finally released her.

He stepped back, blinking, smiling at her unsteady stance. "I just wanted to get that out of the way. For now. See you in thirty."

~ * ~

Trembling, Cassidy waited until he and Jake left before calling the dogs. With trembling legs, she rushed home, undressed Tessa, gave them both a treat and changed clothes. Checking the time, she applied a minimal amount of make-up and wickedly spritzed on a dash of mulberry and cinnamon perfume.

Twenty-eight minutes later she pulled her car up in front of his apartment building. It was a modest, well maintained complex. He'd said he was on the ground floor and she quickly spotted the brown door with a number 15 on it. Should she go knock?

Before she could set the brake, his door swung open and he came out. He wore the same faded jeans from the park, molded to firm thighs. He'd changed his green t-shirt to a blue polo shirt that made his eyes pop and sunglasses hung from the V in the shirt, nestled in the curly mat of dark chest hair. She swallowed. How could one man have such a surplus of sex appeal?

"Nice car," he commented, sliding in and giving her a bright smile. "I like the little doggie nose prints. Good touch." He tapped the glass with his knuckle. "Like happy little kids leaving their sticky fingerprints behind."

"Thanks, I guess." She hadn't gotten around to washing their nose and paw prints off just yet, compliments from the trip to the groomer last week. It was part of her inheritance laundry list, baths and grooming every three weeks. At the way things were going for her, by the time she cleaned them off, it would be time for their next appointment.

"I used to have a Jeep, years ago. My dog loved riding in it and he'd leave big, sloppy nose prints all over the glass." He gave a wistful sigh. "I sure miss old Blackie."

The soft sound tugged at her as pictures formed in her mind. "Blackie?"

"Yeah, he was a bear sized mix of black lab and Great Dane. He was my best buddy for ten years." He shot her a grin. "Now I have Jake."

Ethan's smile warmed her. His affection for his dog reached out and tapped her on the heart. He smelled so good, distracting her from the task ahead. Musk and spices and clean healthy male. What a combination. She pictured a tropical island, with ocean breezes, white cotton clouds, wispy green plants and trees and Ethan sprawled on a hammock, sipping an umbrella drink. With her lying next to him, sharing that drink. And kisses. Dancing on the sand. Under the stars.

"Ready?" she asked quickly, clearing her throat.

"Yep. So how'd you come to work as Midland's city planner?" He leaned back, elbow resting on the window frame, emitting male pheromones like rays of sunshine. She could just bask in them forever.

"My family was from Midland. My sisters and I were raised here. My dad used to always say if you don't like things, be the one to push for change. I came back here after college and found, as an adult, Midland wasn't what I liked. Rather than moving away from my sisters, I decided to push for changes. The position opened up." She paused, giving a wistful sigh. "I used to think it was tailor made for me."

"Not so much now?"

"No, not so much." She wagged her head and pulled over. "How about we start here?"

They exited the car. Cassidy carried a notebook and small camera. Ethan stood protectively next to her as she snapped pictures of love padlocks and made a note of their locations. Taking her elbow, they walked a couple blocks, gathered information on a few more and returned.

"Well, this isn't so bad, locating them all this way," Cassidy decided, unlocking the car.

"Umm, don't rush too much. We have all day." Ethan slid his sunglasses on.

The look was breathtaking. Already handsome, the aviator style dark lenses transformed his features into a carefree boy-on-the-town. Her heart sang at the image. Today was going to be a great day.

~ * ~

Ethan could not imagine spending a day any better than riding around town with Cassidy. Her car, a sporty red Beemer, fit the image of her job, and she handled it like a pro. She was dressed in another power outfit, grey this time, with a cream blouse and heeled shoes with a thick wedge. Instead of coiling her hair in the style he was used to seeing it, she let it hang in a loose, flowing ponytail. It surprised him how much he liked her in a ponytail. He'd never cared for ponytails before, thinking it more for younger girls. On her, it looked carefree and mature. Plus she left the red hat behind. Her perfume was intoxicating enough to make him want to drink it from the bottle.

Her smile made his heart beat fast, her laugh made his pulse gallop and the two, combined, made him weak in the knees. He had thought that kissing her before they started out would have satisfied his crazy impulses. Not the case. Watching her lips, either pulled into a thoughtful pout or lifted in a laughing smile, he felt a kick to his heart. As gentle as coming from a football player.

Remembering the sweet taste of her berry lip gloss she wore at the park only made him ache to kiss her again. And soon. But she was all business now.

True to his expectations, she was dedicated, careful to catalogue photos and notes as they made their way about town. He was doubly glad he offered to come along, to keep a watchful eye out as she made her observations.

"What's your personal opinion of the Love Locks?" he asked, toying with one as she snapped photos.

She made some notes, street names and landmarks he guessed, before looking back at him. "I think the sentiment is pretty."

"Like art?"

He made her smile with that. His chest thumped happily at his newfound skill and he remembered her discomfort at the party about the question of love at first sight.

"Maybe," she agreed. "At least with a few of these collections. Yet any form of art, or expression, needs to be managed." She lifted her head to study the sky before returning to him. "If we decide to keep them, they need to be more showcased in designated areas. Like the Wish Walls."

He must have looked puzzled because she explained what they were. "Oh, right. I've seen them around. Some have very emotional or profound comments on them."

Her smile brightened. "I'm kind of partial to them. They were my suggestion. We can stop at one of my favorites if you want to." She waved her pen at the padlocks. "If we can do something similar for these, then it becomes more art and less vandalism."

He felt the frown building on his face. "Is that how King sees them? Vandalism? Something to drive out of the town?"

Her sad stare pegged him. "I wish I knew why you don't seem to like him much. Or the other way around, as you seem to suggest."

And he wished he could tell her. Words formed on his tongue, salty as his strip name, and he dragged them back scant seconds before they spilled out. He checked the time. "It's almost lunch time. Are you hungry yet?" He had never been to this side of town, so he was clueless where to suggest. "Do you have any good recommendations?"

"A few. Do you like bistros?"

Chapter Thirteen

Cassidy ran the spoon through her creamy broccoli soup, fishing the green chunks out. Across from her, Ethan worked through his hoagie sandwich. Between them sat a basket of French fries and a small plate of catsup.

"Not hungry?" Ethan asked.

"Umm, yes. Just lost in thought."

He took a fry and drowned it in the catsup plate. "About?"

She smiled. His appetite was something else. "Lots of stuff."

"Like?"

"You and Mayor King. It's bugging me. I get the feeling you think he's a power freak."

"Isn't he?"

She shook her head. "Hardly. We still have a council. Adam Gaines, my boss, is the council manager."

Ethen took another bite. "So King is your boss's boss?"

Okay, that didn't come out like she had hoped it would. "What I'm saying is the mayor can't just race through town, waving his fist like an iron club and doing what he wants. There are policies and procedures in place. We have governing bodies, namely the council, and the voting public, who have voices he has to listen to."

"Yep, and in the end, he still does what he wants."

Her shoulders slumped at the grain of truth in his words. "Not always," she feebly protested.

"But sometimes? Occasionally? Enough to infuriate those who work for him?"

"Are you always this intrusive? Prying?" *Accurate?*

He slathered another fry in the catsup, chewed it and picked up the sandwich again. "Sometimes. When I think it's worth the effort." His eyes sought hers, freezing her. "And, Cassidy, today has taught me one thing for sure…you are completely worth my effort."

Her heart trip-hammered as her pulse skipped and heat raced over her skin. The animosity between him and King no longer mattered, pushed recklessly aside by a sudden need. There was no mistaking the hungry look in his ocean blue eyes. If they were not in the public bistro, she'd swear he'd rip his shirt off, and then take hers off.

And suddenly, she wished they were back at her place, alone. She looked around, seeking a distraction, something to bring her back to reality. Before she did something rash. "Do you like chess?" she asked spontaneously.

"Sure, though it's been probably five years since I've played it."

She smiled, and pushed her bread bowl aside. "Not a problem. Come on."

Cassidy stopped to check two more neighborhoods, noting the piles of padlocks, snapping a few photos and making a few notations. Ethan watched and she could sense his building curiosity.

"So how did you come to know this town so well?" Ethan asked after they returned to the car. "It's pretty big. Bigger than I had realized."

She grinned. "It's part of my job to know the town. We have countless maps in the office and more on the computers. As a planner, I am frequently being approached by people all over the city, and I have to be knowledgeable about the areas they are discussing."

He nodded, remaining silent. She wondered what he was thinking, and again wondered at his position at the newspaper. Reporting of most any type could safely be ruled out, since he wasn't very familiar with areas beyond their immediate neighborhoods.

"So here we are." She parked the car in a parallel space and set the lock. "You're going to like this." Impulsively taking his hand, she led him to another park. She enjoyed the feel of his warm palm curled in hers. This park was not a designated dog park like the one they enjoyed,

84

it was geared more for the humans.

"Wonderland Park?" He read the scrolled sign over the archway, flanked by tall bushes.

She giggled at his perplexed expression. "You'll see." Tugging, she led him in, past the kiddie games of teeter-totter, merry-go-round, slides, swings and climbing towers. Children skipped rope and played hopscotch, never bothering to look up from their games. Watchful parents on benches gave them a questioning eye until they walked by. The children's laughter followed them.

Small tables flanked a tennis court. No players were on the court but old men in patched sweaters sat at the tables, idly playing checkers. One smoked a cigar, the odor lifting into the air.

They passed a row of benches. One lone woman sat, reading a newspaper, slowly flipping pages. Warm sunshine spilled down on them. Birds chirped and flew from trees. A couple of picnickers, young lovers on a stolen tryst, sprawled on their plaid blankets, a wicker basket beside them. Two young women stretched out under a huge tree, both reading books. One turned pages on her electric reader and one listened through the earbuds she wore. Joggers swept by them, chatting among their own little group.

"Wow, will you look at that." Ethan slammed to a halt, eyes growing large as he studied the chess field trimmed by low evergreen bushes. Black and white tiled squares a foot square alternated on the close-cropped grass. Fiberglass chess pieces, as tall as three feet, stood in ready places on the giant board.

"Pretty neat, huh?"

Ethan pushed on the queens. "It's heavier than it looks." He examined the piece. "Weighted. But not enough to become wobbly. Very clever."

"So, do you want to be black?" Cassidy moved around to a two foot tall white pawn and nudged it with her foot.

"You're on." Smiling broadly, he moved his e2 pawn up a space.

She slid her bishop over to d3. Pausing only a moment, he dragged the knight over to f6. Cassidy moved another pawn. So did he.

"Ha, first capture!" she crowed as she tapped his pawn with hers and walked it off the board onto the grass.

"Nice. But watch this."

Too late she saw her error. He pushed his queen over to a4.

"Check, Cassidy."

Darn. She had no pieces able to defend so she needed to move the king, and there was only one place she could move him to. Grabbing his fiberglass crown, she kneed him over one square and stood, hands on her hips to study her predicament. And his obvious, and sexy, amusement. "You're pretty good at this," she observed.

He shrugged as he walked around the board, examining pieces. "It's all coming back to me, but that was honestly a lucky move. It's different to visualize moves when you're actually a piece yourself on the board, instead of just looking at it." Leaving his queen, he brought a rook out three squares.

Immediately she blocked with her knight.

He laughed, nodding at her move. "Tricky. I like your style." He moved another pawn up one square to cover the rook from her attack.

As they drifted around the board, moving the pieces, each capturing some and laughing at their animated actions, it was clear he played offensively and she played defensively. While he liked her style, she had to admire his strategy. Using only a few select pieces, and limited moves, he placed her in check twice. She used far more pieces, lost a couple more and seemed more spread out over the board. And she yet had to get him into check.

Wait. She saw a move. Did he even notice? Heart thumping, she walked around the board, checking all angles. She cut him a few glances as he stood there, hands in his pockets, following her movement.

"I have a feeling that I'm missing something here," he finally said.

She nodded, taking hold of her bishop. "You are." She took out his knight and braced herself against the bishop, throwing him a broad smile. "Check. And Checkmate."

"What? Wait. It's not mate. Is it?" Circling the board, he stopped in front of her, taking her into his arms. "Good game, Cassidy. I concede to your superior move." Dropping a kiss to her lips, he tangled his fingers in her hair, sending sizzles of electricity through her.

"And I willingly submit myself to whatever plans you have now that you have captured me."

"Don't you mean your king?" she asked breathlessly, lost in his dark gaze.

"Maybe."

His low murmur lit a fire of a different kind deep inside her. She felt the flames lick to life and grow. His strong, tense body, pressed so close to her, fed the blaze. He was surrendering? What could she possibly do to him?

The cheery melody of an ice cream truck broke between them. Pulling her attention from his smoldering gaze, she watched the same white van with big, bright dots pull up nearby and park.

"Care for a cone?"

Yes, she needed something cold right now. Ice cold. In lieu of a freezing shower, ice cream would do. Mutely, she nodded. He took her elbow and guided her over to the truck. She ordered butter pecan and he requested chocolate fudge, handing out a couple bills.

"Come over here, I'd like to share something with you," he requested as they turned away from the truck.

~ * ~

Ethan wasn't sure what made him need to do this. It was sort of crazy. However, after that game of chess, he was stimulated, in a few ways. The ice cream truck's timing was both excellent and terrible.

They settled on the bench, warm sunshine covering them. She licked her cone, watching him expectantly. He swallowed, forcing his eyes from her sweet mouth to her eyes.

"Okay, you'd said perfect honesty and no secrets. So I think I need to share something important."

Her face lit up and she lowered the cone. He about died when she licked her lower lip, cleaning the sweet stuff away. He coughed.

"I was engaged last year. We'd been in a serious relationship for a while, and marriage seemed like the next logical step."

She cut a glance to his left hand and back up. "You say you were. What happened?"

"We had it all planned. A big event, catered meal, rented dee jay, the whole works. We wanted to do this right. She'd picked out a nice gown, we had the bridesmaids and groomsmen lined up and lots of guests."

Her face paled. "How lovely," she said dryly. "What happened? Did it rain?"

He gave a mirthless laugh, almost harsh. "Sort of. She never showed up. The day of the wedding, I waited at the altar, with music playing and everyone waiting. After a while I got a bad feeling, right here." He placed a fist to his gut. "Then her sister showed up with a note. Rather than just handing it to me, she read it aloud to the whole place."

Her mouth had pulled into an O and her eyes widened in astonishment. "What did it say?"

"That she wasn't going to do this, it had been fun and now she was going back."

Cassidy blinked. "That's sort of vague. Going back to what?"

"Or who? Her previous life. Her previous lover. Turns out I was just a period of distraction for her. A hiatus from her normal happy life. She needed a sucker to play around with and I was handy."

She shook her head, her face a mixture of confusion and outrage. If he weren't so full of self-loathing, he'd appreciate her anger.

"I bought into her act, thought we had something real, and in the end, was played the fool." Boy, was he ever. "So I walked away from that day a shattered mess. But it taught me two things."

"What are they?"

He raised two fingers. "One, go slow in any future relationship, don't get caught being a fool again. And two, adopt a dog."

Chapter Fourteen

Cassidy stared, trying to process his story. It seemed unfathomable someone could do that to another person. Cruel did not adequately describe such a sick mind. And to deliberately cause that sort of pain to a nice guy like Ethan. Why, it was almost criminal.

Ethan was sensitive, honest and obviously a little too trusting. At least he had been. What kind of damage had this unknown woman done to him?

"Why did you tell me this?"

He lifted a shoulder in a shrug and took a bite of his cone. "Because I felt I owed you some honesty about me."

"Fair enough." She felt as if he'd just handed her a precious gift. One she had no clue what to do with.

She took the last few bites of her cone and wiped her hands. "I suppose we should get back to work. There is more city for us to cover."

Standing first, Ethan reached for her hand and helped her up, drawing her close to him. His kiss would be cold and chocolatey. She could already taste him in her mind and readied herself for his touch.

He stroked the back of his finger down her cheek. "Thank you for bringing me along. It was a great game of chess."

He drew back, releasing her. He breathed in a deep breath, rammed his hands into his pockets and headed for her car. Taken aback, Cassidy followed. Inside the car, he pulled the sunglasses back on and waited for her.

They cruised a few streets, her hands tight on the wheel, her mind trying to make sense of Ethan. Why didn't he kiss her right then? He'd shared an incredibly personal and intimate detail from his life, had her in his arms, and then commented on chess. Really?

Giving up, she shook her head and parked the car. "Now, we see more crime in this area than any other throughout the city and we've been looking into different forms of public lighting as a better deterrent." She waved at some light poles. "While we're here, I need to include the current lighting and later I can compare it to our crime reports for the last few months. Maybe we can find a suitable solution."

"I can see where that would be important. This is mostly residential, not too affluent, and all voters."

Her lips thinned at his subtle jab to Mayor King. Honestly, what was it with those two? Would King tell her if she asked him?

They strolled along, and she made copious notes of public lighting as well as public expression forms. Ethan stayed a few feet away, watchful and quiet as he studied the area. She'd give up ice cream if only she knew what he was thinking behind that impassive mask.

And the real kicker was, he still looked oh-so-sexy, even behind the deadpan face and dark lenses. His toned physique, which she knew to be firm and warm under her fingers, looked to die for in worn jeans and tight shirt.

Stumbling, she caught herself on a light pole, nearly dropping her stuff.

"Hey, you okay?" Ethan caught her with one hand and scooped up her camera and notebook with the other. She saw the concern in his eyes through the tinted lenses and embarrassment swept over her.

"Yes, fine. I didn't see the rut in the sidewalk." She kicked at it with the toe of her shoe. What a convenient little fault to find.

"Yeah, someone should do something to fix the sidewalks around town. Some have craters big enough to swallow a person."

She tried for a laugh. "I doubt they're that large."

"Well, maybe not quite. Certainly, large enough to consume a cat at least."

She nodded. "Come to one of the public meetings and bring it up to the council. Mention specific neighborhoods that need repair and we can probably get it bid on and scheduled before too long."

He made a noise that sounded like a cross between a grunt and a laugh. "I'll see what I can do about that."

His expression and tone did not sound promising so she gave up with a shrug. He could attend if he wanted to. If not, he had no room to complain. 'Be the change' was her manta. "There is another Wish Wall near here. I'd like to stop and see what is new."

He held her elbow cupped in his palm, escorting her down the street for another block. The tall structure, this one standing just over seven feet high, greeted them as they rounded the corner. It had been at least a couple months since Cassidy had last been to this one. Ethan released his hold and she stood, studying the colorful chalk messages. Ethan moved a few feet over, rocking back on his heels and hands in his pockets as he read them as well.

She heard him chuckle at some and she smiled at a few herself.

"I like this person," Ethan said, pointing a finger to a sentence written in green chalk. "He or she wants to become mayor of Midland."

Sure enough. *When I grow up I want to be Midland's best mayor.*

Great.

Moving over, she read other notes. Drawn to a familiar handwriting, she paused and stepped closer, slowly reading the long letter. As the words penetrated her heart, her jaw dropped. Suddenly weak, she pressed her hand to the wall's cool surface, and ran her trembling fingers under the final words.

Before I die... I am dying. Soon. And I'm scared. I'm even more scared for my sister. She's never found love yet and I fear she never will. She uses work as a substitute. My hope is that by giving her my dogs, they will teach her to love others and they can be an open door to that love—whatever it might be. I want to live, sure, but more than that, I want my sisters to be happy and loved. There is nothing better than a little dog or two to show even the most stubborn heart the joys of love.

It ended with a yellow smiley face, almost as a silent signature. Except Cassidy didn't need a name. Hot tears spilled down her cheeks. Her chest burned. Cindy. Who else could it be? She'd even drawn small paw prints in chalk, one pair in pink and the other in blue.

Ethan's arms wrapped around her and she folded into his hug, sobs shaking her.

"That's why she gave me the dogs," she cried, understanding dawning like the sun's rays. Even as she was dying, her baby sister was thinking of her future.

She heard Ethan's heart beat at her ear and closed her eyes, taking comfort from his reassuring, steady rhythm. Love. She tasted the salty tears on her lips. Felt his warm arms enveloping her, drawing her into a cocoon he spun. Safe. She trembled, weak against the onslaught of emotions. He stroked her hair, patting softly. Gentle.

Love. Safe. Gentle. Reassuring. Warm. Soft.

All words to describe Ethan. And she'd add patient, understanding, honest and compassionate.

But did she love him? What did she feel for him? She knew how he felt. All of those things and more. But what did her heart feel for him? Love, which Cindy tried so hard for her to find?

She smiled mirthlessly. Would she even know love if she tripped over a manhole cover and fell face first into it?

"Feeling better?"

She blinked and lifted her face to Ethan. His tentative smile knocked at her heart better than tripping over a manhole cover. Doubtlessly mascara was running down her face in streams of black but he gave no indication of noticing.

She nodded and pulled away just enough to swipe at her nose. He dug around and produced a tissue. Grateful, she wiped tears and mascara away.

"Better. Thank you." She stuffed the damp tissue in her pocket. Ethan lifted her camera and snapped a photo of Cindy's message and handed it back to her.

"You might want to see that again."

It felt burned in her heart and soul, but he was probably right. She could also show it to Karen. And they could binge on ice cream.

Pulling the notebook and camera to her chest, she dragged her gaze off the wall and turned back to Ethan. His patient, compassionate expression touched her, warming her, chasing away the chills of moments ago.

Heat spread over her as his gentle look softened, growing hot with a sudden desire, matching hers. The shift from grief to want struck her like a bolt of white lightning, taking her breath.

"What are you thinking right now, Cassidy?"

She boldly met his eyes. "I was wishing this assignment was done because I want to see if my fantasies of us are as good as the real thing."

His smile was slow, cautious, building up to reach his eyes. His touch was electric, sending red sizzles of warmth radiating through her. "Darling, there is only one way to find out. Let's get this town wrapped up."

Chapter Fifteen

"I think we've canvased the entire town." Cassidy turned the car onto another street that would lead them home. She cut a shy glance at Ethan. Since her bold announcement, he'd remained the perfect gentleman by escorting her back to the car and remaining protective as she rushed through the last few sections on her list. However, she sensed a slow growing pensiveness. He said very little, watched her with a new scrutiny and now seemed to have wandered off mentally.

He nodded at her comment, glancing at the notebook and camera that sat between them. "I've never seen so much of Midland. I honestly had no idea it was this big."

"So you're not from here?"

"No. I was raised in Connecticut. Moved to New York for college. Drifted a few places afterward, until I came west and landed here. It could be a nice place to raise a family."

Was he suggesting he'd want to raise a family? Or just that anyone could do so nicely here? "California must seem like a different world from Connecticut and New York?" She turned the car onto a road that would circle around and take them back to her place faster.

"At first it was. I adjusted." He lifted a shoulder in an absent shrug. "So, you're okay with me going back to your place? Still?"

Was that what was worrying him? "I'm still okay with it. Are you?"

He gave a tight nod.

"Well, we're about fifteen minutes away, just in case you need time to take a little blue pill."

Startled, he gave a short chuckle. "Don't worry, Cassidy, that is not something I deal with."

Parking a short while later, she turned off the ignition.

"What will your doorman think?"

His question took her by surprise. "He probably won't think anything at all. He knew you came over that one morning. Now we're coming back together. It could be for any reason and I doubt he will even consider it."

He looked around the parking deck, appeared about to say something and must have thought better of it. Wordlessly, he came around to her side of the car and cupped her elbow, guiding her past the front entry and to the elevators. In her recent fantasy, he pushed her against the wall once the door slid shut, plying his lips over hers and working the buttons on her blouse.

In reality, the door slid closed and he stood, hands rammed into his pockets, waiting as they rose to her floor. She might have appreciated that more if they were sharing the elevator with others, which they were not.

Entering her place, she set her things aside just as the dogs launched a full scale welcome. Remi flew to Ethan, spinning, leaping and woofing in canine glee. Tessa sat, butt wiggling eagerly, as she waited her turn for pats and scratches.

Fleetingly Cassidy wondered if she needed to join the line. Ethan finished greeting the dogs and stood, brushing himself off. Cassidy stood, hands curled around the back of the nearest chair, heart thudding. A warm shiver rippled all the way to her toes as their eyes met.

"So, you had said something earlier about a fantasy?"

He was shy. The revelation shocked her. She'd never met a man who was awkward about foreplay. She'd assumed they were pretty much born with the necessary skills. Well, it's not like she had loads of personal experience either. Just her daydreams born out of lonely nights.

Smiling, she advanced a step, closing the gap between them. Reaching out, she pulled his sunglasses free of his shirt and placed them on the counter. Holding his eyes, she worked her hands under his polo shirt, dragging her fingertips over his taut stomach muscles. He inhaled sharply. She lightly tugged a bit of curly chest hair, smiling as he closed his eyes.

She kicked out of her wedges and stepped on his sneakers, tilting her lips up to his, while bending his head down to meet her. They kissed. She tasted the salami, provolone and sweet cola from his lunch. Once he relaxed, she released him, stepping aside but dragging her fingers down to hold his hands.

"This way," she beckoned, pulling him to the living room. Scents of vanilla greeted them as she eased him down on the sofa. Bending one leg on the sofa, she straddled his thigh with her other leg, biting her lip in anticipation. Butterflies took off in her belly and warmth spread over her.

Uttering a low growl, he gently flipped on top of her, spreading his arms on either side. She gripped his arms, tight like iron, and met his intense stare, hungry heat filling her.

"Are you sure about this, Cassidy?"

Mutely, she nodded. She'd never been so sure of anything before.

He lowered himself for one long kiss, plunging deep into her mouth. Excitement ricocheted through her as his knee moved between her legs. Burning heat pulsed through her like lava. Desire knifed over her, nearly cutting her in two.

She gasped, crying his name, meeting his kiss with her own hunger.

Suddenly, Ethan backed away. Breaking all contact, he stood up, and ran his fingers through his hair. He gave her a look laden with remorse, shaking her to her core.

"Ethan?" Ice cold water dumped over her.

He shook his head, taking a couple steps back. "I can't do this, Cassidy. Not right now. It's not fair to you."

Plucking his sunglasses from the counter, he spun and all but sprinted for the door. He gripped the handle, looked back at her, that same rueful look etched deeply on his face. "I am so sorry, Cassidy."

The hollow click of the handle echoed through the room as she sat there, head swimming with confusion, her nerves still jerking with unfulfilled need. What just happened?

~ * ~

"Dad? It's Ethan." Ethan gripped the phone, his chest tight. Would he remember who he was? "How you doing, Dad?"

"Fine, just fine."

His dad sounded so frail, his breath coming in labored pants, like a dog who ran too long. His COPD must be worse today. So how was his dementia? He worked up the courage to ask. "What's going on, Dad?"

"Not much. Got a new television set. The shows are really something." He chuckled.

"Yeah, I bet they are." The nursing home staff must have replaced his old set. Or just replaced tapes of old shows with different ones. "So, Dad, I have a problem. Do you remember the comic strip I draw? *Punch?* There's a woman who needs to know it's me drawing it. Her boss is badgering her to find out."

"You'll never shine if your light is under a bushel."

"Maybe. But it's safer for me this way. And I like this woman, Dad. I really like her. We could have something good if my secret identity wasn't between us."

"Sounds like quite a problem. What do you want to do about it?"

Ethan raked his hair, blowing out a breath. "I don't know, Dad, that's why I called you. I was hoping you'd have good advice for me. You used to always have advice for me, even when I didn't want to hear it."

"My wife used to hate secrets. Even when it was something for her birthday. She had to know everything."

Dread rolled over Ethan, along with a cold chill. What an odd choice of words. He forced a smile. "Yep, Mom sure was a looker."

"I'm sorry, but who is this?"

His heart twisting, Ethan politely ended the conversation. He dropped the phone and sank down next to Jake, burying his face in the dog's furry neck.

~ * ~

"Hey, boss, got a second?" Ethan rapped at the doorframe. Charles looked up from his computer screen.

"Yeah, come on in." He waved him in.

Ethan glanced around the cluttered room, full of plaques, stacks of papers, old soda cans and Chinese food containers. Charles must collect his mail down at Egg Foo Yong.

"What's up, kid?" He picked up a soda can and pulled the tab, tossing it onto a pile of dozens of others.

Ethan pushed stuff out of his way so he could reach the chair more or less across from Charles. The whole room reminded him of the journalist's towering and overflowing desks from the *Shoe* comic strip.

He dropped his elbows to his knees. "Why'd we start using the Salty Kidd instead of just using my real name?"

"For the strip?" Charles set the can aside, onto a stack of papers like a paperweight.

"Yes." How many places did Charles think he used the pseudonym?

"It was cheaper than the witness protection plan. Why?"

"I'm thinking of sharing my identity with someone." He drew in a breath. "Someone who works at Mayor King's palace."

Charles, midway of reaching for another cola stopped, gaping at Ethan. He looked like a fish out of water. Ethan half expected him to fall to the floor in another moment. Would 9-1-1 even be able to get into the crowded room?

"Ethan, *The Gazette* can't be responsible if you do." Charles found his voice. "In case of harm. To you."

Ethan nodded. "I understand." He started to stand up. "Hey, if something suddenly happens to me, don't let Mitch get my dog."

~ * ~

"Cassidy, got a minute?"

Adam caught her coming out of the breakroom. Eying the newspaper folded under his arm, she clutched the coffee-to-go in her hand and feigned a smile. It probably looked more like a grimace. "Yes, sure."

He fell into step with her as she headed down the hall to her office. "Have you seen the paper yet?"

"Today's? No. Is there something important in there?" Their small talk was starting to remind her of the final words prisoners get to say before they meet their end. Without waiting for an answer, she switched topics. "Did you get that neighborhood breakdown for the survey?"

They reached her office and she stepped behind the desk, preferring to remain standing. Adam unfolded the paper, holding it out to page four. *Punch* glared back at her, automatically galling her.

"Adam, honestly, I—"

She looked up at him, ready to apologize for her failure to find the culprit behind the festering strip, when she felt her eyes pulled back down to the picture. Narrowing her gaze, the air escaped her chest and her lips parted in astonishment.

A car, a convertible, long and elegant, rambled down the street, dragging an assortment of padlocks behind it. Some locks bore initials and a few held mini sketches of unhappy faces. She could almost make out her own in the jangle of padlocks. She scanned the initials on the various locks, finding one that read C.G. + E. S. A city limit sign crowded the corner of the scene. Swinging her gaze back to the car, sitting behind the wheel, happily driving the love locks out of town, was a stick figure image of a padlock, with the suggested impression of none other than Mayor I. R. King. Smiling broadly, he waved an iron club in his stick figure fist.

The paper fell from her fingers as she fought to draw in a breath. *Ethan.*

He had to be the Salty Kidd.

Chapter Sixteen

"Thank goodness you're here." Cassidy lifted the paper bags, shaking them. "I brought ice cream and stuff."

Karen reached for a bag with one hand and propelled Cassidy inside with the other. "What are we celebrating?" she asked as they headed for the kitchen.

The younger child lay napping. The next one up in age sat on a foam mat, playing with foam blocks. Seeing her, he waddled over, arms outstretched. She couldn't even remember their names. God, she was a mess. "We're commiserating."

"Oh-oh." Karen plopped the carton of ice cream down, studying Cassidy with narrowed eyes. "What happened? Something to do with Ethan?"

Tears, so barely controlled up until now, forced past her thread bare resolve. Bag sliding, she dropped into a chair, shoulders slumped, not able to meet her sister's eyes.

"Did you get fired? What happened?" She sat down, opposite Cassidy and helped the child climb into her lap. As if by magic, a wafer cookie appeared and she offered it to the toddler. "Here you go, sweetie," she said before turning her focus back to Cassidy, handing over a tissue. "Now talk to me."

"King blew up at the latest cartoon. Adam is furious. He said I wasn't taking this seriously enough, and jeopardizing King's reelection chances," she gushed, swiping at tears. "He put me on suspension until I can get my priorities straight."

Karen tossed her free arm into the air. "How absurd! You're doing what you can do. They can't expect you to pull a name from the air. If Ethan doesn't want to share—"

"It's Ethan."

"Right. It comes down to Ethan. No one can force him to—"

Cassidy gripped Karen's arm, hiccupping. "Ethan is the Salty Kidd."

Karen drew back, her mouth pulled into an O and her eyes widened. "Your Ethan? He told you that?"

Her Ethan. The incredulous words pierced her heart, going deep. "Not in words." She shook her head. His picture was better than a thousand words.

"So how do you know? What did he say?"

Cassidy looked around. Spotting a newspaper lying on the end table, she nodded toward it. "Is that today's *Gazette*?" At Karen's confirmation, she walked over to scoop it up. Hand trembling, she flipped to the page, heart beating fast knowing what she would find.

Gazing at it for a moment, she looked for any other way to interpret it that would not point the finger squarely back at Ethan. Finding none, she folded it over and handed it to Karen.

"We were out driving around town," she explained. "He was helping me with research work for King and we discussed King and the locks. Something was said about him driving them out of the town and waving an iron club."

"Well, that does sort of look like the Mayor's car. In a cartoonish kind of way."

Cassidy blew out a breath, at a loss for words. How could one stupid cartoon so completely ruin her life? And to know it was drawn by Ethan. Oh, she buried her head in her hands.

"Sweetie, take this and go back to your blocks, okay?" Karen produced another wafer cookie and sent the toddler back to the foam mat. Getting up, she took the bags to the counter, pulled two dishes from the dish drainer and dropped big scoops of ice cream in. Smothering them with layers of chocolate syrup, butterscotch and whipped cream, she plunked one in front of Cassidy. Sitting down again, she scooted the other bowl closer.

"Eat up before it melts. Did you tell your boss?"

"Are you kidding? And say what? So, Adam, it turns out this hunky, sexy guy I've been seeing lately is really the mastermind artist behind *Punch.* You don't mind if I keep seeing him while he single handedly destroys our Mayor—our boss's—political career? Lately I've been thinking he might be the one, so I don't want this little issue to come between us and my job here either. You're good with all this, right, Adam?" She jeered, hiccupping again. "Somehow I don't think that conversation would go over well."

"No, probably not when presented like that. You'd most likely end up worse than suspended." Karen took another bite. "So what do you plan to do?"

Cassidy took a bite, letting the smooth syrup and cold ice cream melt on her tongue before swallowing. Chocolate could do so much. Doctors should write prescriptions for this instead of medications. "I don't know."

"Fair enough. What does Ethan have to say for himself?"

Cassidy nodded to the paper, folded and resting at Karen's elbow, another bite slowly melting in her mouth.

"You mean you haven't talked since this came out? Oh, Cassidy, you have to go see him. Talk to him, confront him, see what he has to say in his defense."

"I'd rather eat chocolate ice cream."

"After you eat that. Cassidy, really, you need to discuss this. Does he know how this thing of his is impacting your career?"

"Sort of."

Karen blew out a breath and shook her head. "Catch him up to speed, Cass."

"After another bowl."

"Nope, now. Gimme." Standing up, she swept the bowl out from under Cassidy, leaving her holding an empty spoon. Taking her bowl too, she placed both in the sink. "Love you, sis, now go see Ethan."

~ * ~

Cassidy stood outside Ethan's door, dread and anger curled inside her like multi-colored ribbons. Shifting from one foot to the other, she

102

inhaled and lifted a hand to knock. She still had no clue what she was going to say.

Jake barked. He must have sensed it was her because his tempo changed just before Ethan opened the door.

"I ought to punch you."

The words tumbled from her mouth without thought. Okay, so anger was the winning thread. She stood straight, meeting his solemn nod.

"You would have every right."

"Why didn't you tell me?"

He looked even more miserable, if that were possible. "I wanted to."

"Was someone holding your tongue prisoner?"

He motioned Jake aside and opened the door further. "Would you like to come in?"

She crossed her arms over her chest, jutting her chin out. "I'm not sure."

"Cassidy, I can't tell you how many times I wanted to just open up, tell you it was me. But you have to understand it was a condition of my job. Only a handful of *Gazette* employees know what I do there, who I really am."

"Good for you. Because I have been suspended from my job. Pending review, I probably won't have it much longer."

His eyes widened and his jaw dropped. "All because of this? Just because you couldn't tell them who the Salty Kidd was?" His incredulous indignation almost matched Karen's.

"Yes." She nodded. "Mayor King is really taking this seriously and your latest attack has all but destroyed his chances at reelection."

"He's an attackable guy."

"Nonetheless, he's my boss. He's your mayor. And now, because I have allowed you to continue your antics, I am soon going to be out of a job. I hope you still see something funny in there."

"Cassidy—"

Hand out, she whirled, anger unfurling in her. She rammed a finger in his face. "Just stay out of my life. You've done enough damage." Her heels beat a rapid tattoo as she returned to her car. Only after she rounded the block did she slap the steering wheel and allow the tears to fall.

~ * ~

Cassidy awoke, groaned and flopped the pillow over her face. The sunlight shining beyond her curtain made a mockery of the suspension looming ahead. What was she going to do all day without a job to go to? And tomorrow?

She could go see Ethan. They could try talking about this since her anger had cooled a few degrees.

"Or not."

Beside her, Tessa stirred at her voice, stretching and inching just a tiny bit closer, placing her paw on Cassidy's arm.

"Are you sorry I'm out of a job or just sorry because you won't see Ethan again?"

Remi leaped up, tail wagging and tongue lolling in eager anticipation. Cassidy threw back the covers.

"Okay, fine. Let me get up and we'll go to the park. But I'm letting you know right now, if Ethan is there, we are leaving. Got it?"

Not needing to dress for work, she pulled a pair of sweatpants from the box of Cindy's things and tugged them on. Exchanging her shirt for another one, she slipped on her sneakers. Leashing the dogs, she pocketed just her keys and swung the door open. A couple of blocks later, she pulled them to a stop outside the gate, surveying the crowd for Ethan's tall silhouette or Jake running with his pack of friends. Seeing neither, she unhooked their leashes.

"I mean it, come back here immediately if I call you."

With echoing barks, they were gone, chasing each other across the grass. Too restless to sit, she paced around the entrance, keeping an eye out in case Ethan and Jake came along. She was either going to have to confront him some day or find another park.

~ * ~

"Whoa, buddy, hold on a sec." Ethan pulled back on Jake's leash. Up ahead was Cassidy, with her dogs doing a decent impression of a heel. Her back was to him and she was dressed in sweats and a t-shirt, but he would know her from any angle. There was no forgetting her butt or shapely legs. Her hair was messed and he doubted she'd even combed it yet. Had she brushed her teeth?

Fresh guilt settled on him, adding to the weight of the anguish that had kept him awake all night. He was pretty sure he could never feel lower or worse than he already did. Seeing her dressed in sloppy sweats added weight to his already heavy guilt till he thought his back might break.

Settling on a bench, he watched the dogs. What was he going to do? How could he make this up to Cassidy and get her job back?

Ten minutes later he had a plan. Bold and brash, it was guaranteed to succeed or get him jailed, or both. Probably both.

"Come on, Jake." Back home, he hung up the leash and gave Jake a big bone. "That will keep you busy, buddy, just in case I don't get back home right away. Uncle Mitch might have to come pay my bail and he's not all that quick. Be a good boy." With a final pat, he grabbed his jacket and was out the door.

He'd always thought most mayors had their offices inside city hall. Not I. R. King. He had a separate building adjacent to the public offices, connected by a translucent ceiling hallway and diamond patterned black and white tiles. Outer lobby and desks protected his inner sanctuary, acting as a buffer to keep undesirables out. No doubt the secretaries and sentries were well paid to ensure only the select few made it through.

Well, today, he was getting in, if he had to break every wall down to do so.

Feeling like he was entering a king's court, which would make him the court jester, Ethan made his way past the posted guard, ignoring his suspicious stare, and made straight for the center desk and the large-bosomed matron seated there. She looked like she could be Attila the Hun's cousin.

She looked up from her computer, studied him a moment and sighed. "Yes."

It didn't sound like a question and he didn't take it as one. She sounded more like he was interrupting something important. Solitaire? He brushed past her irritated glare. "I am here to see Mayor King."

"Do you have an appointment?"

"No. But he will want to see me. I can guarantee it."

Ryan Jo Summers

The guard stiffened, standing straighter on alert. Attila's cousin frowned, lowering her glasses. "The mayor is very busy. He cannot see people who don't make appointments."

Yeah, he'd bet the guy was so busy. Probably getting massages and pedicures. "He will want to see me."

She sighed, this time removing her glasses. Her irritation could not be more obvious. Under normal circumstances, he would have enjoyed this. He loved to irk people like her. Just not now.

"And you are?"

He drew a steady breath. "The Salty Kidd."

Chapter Seventeen

Cassidy flipped through the channels with a bored sigh. She'd already been through the whole menu three times. Nothing changed except the commercials and they were even starting to look the same. Tessa lay on her side, head on her lap. Remi spread out at the other end of the sofa, snoring and his legs twitching.

"At least one of us has some nice action going on," she muttered to Tessa. It had been three days of her suspension and, to be honest, she didn't think she'd survive much longer. Today, once the paper came, she'd start looking for another job. Right after she took a black marker and colored out whatever stupid cartoon Ethan drew this time. She shuddered to think about it.

"And I was really starting to like him too."

She cast a glance to the bouquet of tulips and lilies he had sent her the day after she stormed away from his place. They had not dulled her anger much but she couldn't bear to toss them out. So she changed the water each day, added a crushed aspirin and wondered why Ethan was such a coward he couldn't have told her he was the mastermind behind *Punch* in the first place. Or second. Or third.

What would she have done if he had? Gazing at the colorful blooms, she asked herself that question again. Would she have run to Adam and Mayor King, turning him over for them to do what they wanted to? Would she have kept his secret, and still ended up suspended?

She didn't know. And it hardly mattered now. She was suspended, termination was eminent and, for the moment, she was beyond bored and frustrated.

She'd already pestered Karen until the ice cream and even wafer cookies were gone. In Karen's no-nonsense and tough-love manner, she'd sent her away with a hug and kiss. She'd started taking the dogs to another park, smaller and further away that she had to drive them to, but in the opposite direction. No chance of bumping into him.

The phone rang, and both dogs jumped. She eyed it. Karen? One of the girls from the office? Ethan? Scooping it up, the caller ID belonged to Adam. Her heart skipped a beat. "Oh-oh, here it goes, guys."

"Cassidy. How are you doing?"

She tried to muster up a smile and quickly failed. "I've developed a new appreciation for sweats."

He chuckled, stopping soon. "I'd like for you to come in so we can talk."

"Are you firing me, Adam? If so, I can be fired from the comfort of my sofa and in my sweats."

"Cassidy, just come to my office. One o' clock."

The line went dead in her ear, probably a forerunner of her career. She checked the time. Barely past eleven now. The paper should have been delivered by now. She had time to black out the cartoon and start circling promising classifieds.

~ * ~

Twelve-fifty and Cassidy stood outside Adam's office. She'd already ran into Kelly, who was overjoyed to see her and plied her with several questions. There were big doings going on with Adam and Mayor King, but no one seemed to know what. Lots of closed door meetings.

Cassidy swallowed. Doubtlessly her official termination and severance package. And their plans to replace her. Dana would be a good choice. She would have to mention it to Adam. Sucking in a deep breath, legs shaky, she knocked twice.

Adam swung the door open, a genteel smile on his face. She knew that smile, except it had never been aimed at her before.

"Cassidy, glad you made it. Come in."

Following his lead, she followed, heart thumping. Was King here as well? Glancing around the room, her breath stalled. Seated in a corner chair, a cautious expression on his face, was Ethan.

"Cassidy." He nodded tightly.

She returned his nod, her tongue turned to the same rubbery consistency as her legs. Well, he wasn't in handcuffs, so that was a good sign.

"Please, sit." Adam gestured to a chair near Ethan's. Weakly, she slid into the chair before her legs gave out. Now she was glad she took the time to change from her sweats into a proper business suit. If she were facing the firing squad, and Ethan, she'd rather do it dressed in style.

Adam brought his palms together in a loud clap, making Cassidy jump. Wincing, she pulled her attention from Ethan over to Adam. She'd never known suspense could hang heavy like clouds, or suffocate like smoke. She coughed once.

"Cassidy, your boyfriend here came to see Mayor King and me," he waved at Ethan.

"Ah, he's not my—"

"With a surprising confession," Adam continued over her feeble correction. "And it seems I owe you an apology."

She blinked. "You do?"

"Mr. Sheppard has told us how you pestered him relentlessly to get into *The Gazette*, to find out who that cartoonist was. And how he struggled to keep the facts away from you. I am sorry I didn't believe you when you said you were trying." He sat down. "Now I understand how hard you really did try."

She was speechless. Cutting a glance to Ethan, she raised an eyebrow. He'd exaggerated her efforts. Why?

"And Mr. Sheppard also told us how you begged him, pleaded with him to stop the cartoons. At least to stop aiming them at Mayor King and those who work here or topics related to the city."

They never had that conversation, not like that. How could they have?

"And how you left him in a fit of anger because he refused to listen to you. Does all of that sound pretty much on the mark?"

Well, the last part did sort of. Ethan gave her another solemn look, chilling her. He'd just placed himself on the chopping block—for her. She swallowed. "Y…yes."

"Good. In that case, Cassidy, I am sorry." He dropped his hands to the desk. "When your Mr. Sheppard first came, along with Mayor King, with his admission, I didn't know what to think. I'm still not sure what to think. However, I do know I want you to come back to work. Consider your suspension erased."

She found her voice. "What about *Punch*?" she asked, looking over at Ethan.

"I'll leave you two to discuss that." Adam stood up and headed for the door. Once he was gone, Cassidy whirled to Ethan.

"*Punch* is going away."

She worked that around. "You're quitting?"

"I already gave Charles my two week notice. I gave my word to King and your boss that I will do a series of sketches, ending with the Salty Kidd tipping his hat to the mayor and fine leaders and planners of Midland. And then he's riding into the sunset."

"But what will you do then?" She tried to imagine a world without that cartoon in the paper. Or a day without Ethan. A thread of panic unfurled inside her.

He shrugged. "I can do lots of other stuff. Animation. Graphics. Illustration. I already put a couple resumes out there." Again, he shrugged, getting to his feet. "The bottom line is I can get another job. I can even move away if I have too. Your life is here, Cassidy, and your heart."

Was it? Still? "You did this for me?"

He nodded. "You. And us. I can't bear for you to hate me."

"I never hated you, Ethan." She shook her head. "Yes, I was angry, but I never hated you." Words filled her mouth, fighting to get out. "I wanted us to…."

He knelt at her knee, taking up her hand into his. Warmth spread from him to her, covering her with goosebumps. His deep gaze rolled over her like ocean water. "Cassidy, I would give up anything for you and for us. I want there to be an 'us'. You, me, three dogs and eventually some kids. The Salty Kidd is retiring, never to return, and I will do whatever makes you happy."

Joy exploded through her like fireworks, hot and colorful. "Oh, Ethan!" He took both hands and pulled her up, bringing her close. She smelled his clean, musky scent and minty breath. Her fingers twined into his dark strands.

"Cassidy Grant, I can't offer you a whole lot in regards to material stuff, but I will love you with everything I have. I will be forever faithful, protect and provide to the best of my ability, and always cherish what we have. Will you marry me?"

A startling fact pushed into her tangle of thoughts. Her heart no longer belonged to Midland or her job. If she could visit Karen, David and the kids regularly, she would be happy anywhere, as long as she was with Ethan. Acknowledgement filled her and she smiled, reaching for his lips. "How many kids do you want?"

"As many as you do."

"In that case, yes."

About the author

Ryan Jo Summers is an author who writes across the genres. She pens romance novels blending elements of Inspirational, suspense, mystery, paranormal and time travel in any combination. She covers non-fiction as well as fictional short stories and poetry.

In her spare time, she likes to hang out with her pets, go to the nearby forest and river or gather with friends. She enjoys chess, Mah Jongg, and word-find puzzles, and houseplants. She also likes to cook, creating new recipes from old favorites. If she has any time left over, she paints ceramics and acrylics on canvas. She makes her home in the beautiful mountains of Western North Carolina.

Visit Ryan Jo at her website to sign up for updates on her writing!

Website: www.ryanjosummers.com
Blog: summersrye.wordpress.com
Facebook: facebook.com/pages/Ryan-Jo-Summers-author-
page/312875648810797

www.ingramcontent.com/pod-product-compliance
Lightning Source LLC
Chambersburg PA
CBHW021120130626
46554CB00002B/795